THE PLAINSMAN

After seeing his father set upon and stabbed, nothing will ever be the same for young Will Cody. He kills his first man at the age of ten, and the following years see him fight constant battles — against marauding Cheyenne, the Civil War, the Great Plains themselves, and merciless guerrilla fighters. But even spit-and-grit Will Cody — more famously known as Buffalo Bill — is only human . . . and has he finally met his match?

STEVE HAYES AND
BEN BRIDGES

◆

THE
PLAINSMAN

Complete and Unabridged

LINFORD
Leicester

First published in Great Britain in 2016

First Linford Edition
published 2017

A catalogue record for this book is available
from the British Library.

ISBN 978–1–4448–3484–0

Published by
F. A. Thorpe (Publishing)
Anstey, Leicestershire

Set by Words & Graphics Ltd.
Anstey, Leicestershire
Printed and bound in Great Britain by
T. J. International Ltd., Padstow, Cornwall

This book is printed on acid-free paper

This is for Robbin and Janet

Invention is the surest form of history.

Anonymous

Part One — Yankee Spy

Part One — Yankee Start

1

'*Now!*'

Even as the command left his lips, Clem Butterfield and his equally disheveled companion burst out of the trees, one to either side of the boy on the plow horse.

The boy — he was about eighteen or so — had no time react as Clem grabbed him by the right arm and dragged him sideways off the heavy-set animal. In the same moment his friend, Harvey Trace, grabbed the youngster's left foot and boosted upward to make the job of unseating him even easier.

Their victim described a short arc then hit the loamy soil hard, his ragged-edged palm leaf hat falling from his head. He was dressed poorly in bib overalls and a collarless shirt that had once been white. He didn't look like much of a threat, even with the Lindsay two-shot percussion pistol he'd tucked behind his cracked leather waist belt. But as his startled horse thumped off a few yards, he reached for the pistol with surprising speed.

'*Clem!*' cried Harvey.

Clem was way ahead of him. Moving swiftly given his size, he kicked at the pistol and sent it flying. Then he threw himself onto the boy, his greater weight knocking much of the air and all of the fight out of him. Lights popped in the youngster's skull, and he shook his shaggy blond head to clear it.

Clem, meanwhile, sat up on him, pinned the boy's arms beneath his folded legs, and deftly slid a sword bayonet from his belt. When the boy opened his eyes again, he felt the tip of the weapon prick the skin beneath his chin and immediately froze.

It went deathly quiet in the sun-dappled glade until, seeing the Union blue uniforms his captors wore, the youngster squawked: 'Hold . . . hold up, there, mister! I . . . I'm with you!'

Although he kept the tip of the bayonet tucked firm against the boy's throat, Clem cocked his head like an inquisitive dog. In his twenties, the big soldier's sketchy whiskers were a shade darker than the curly fair hair visible beneath his black-billed forage cap. His eyelashes flickered rapidly as he thought about what his prisoner had just said.

'What-all you mean, you're with us?' he asked.

The boy finally caught his breath. His flushed, oval face was clean-shaven, the brow above his piercing hazel eyes strong and pronounced, his nose a thin, direct line that pointed the way to a narrow but equally intractable mouth.

'Name's . . . name's Will Cody,' he gasped. 'I'm on a . . . a scoutin' mission for . . . General Smith.'

Harvey had scurried back to the bushes to retrieve their weapons — two modified Springfield rifles. Now he reappeared just over his partner's shoulder, a broad-shouldered silhouette against the blue Mississippi sky.

Scratching a weak jaw that looked sore from shaving, he asked doubtfully: 'In them duds?'

'How far d'you . . . think I'd get in . . . uniform?' Will countered testily.

That made his captors think some more.

'You sayin' you're a *spy*, kid?' Clem said in a near-whisper.

Figuring the truth would serve him well right then, Will nodded.

'What's the name of your regiment?'

'Seventh Kansas,' said Will. 'Yours?'

'Seventeenth Illinois,' said Clem. 'Me'n Harvey here got separated from the rest of our outfit after Tupelo.'

Will looked surprised. 'Tupelo? Hell, we fought that battle weeks ago!'

'Yeah, an' we been tryin' to get back to our outfit ever since,' said Clem, without much conviction.

Unless Will missed his guess, these two were more likely to be deserters, pure and simple. They'd fled the field of battle, gotten themselves hopelessly lost and somehow ended up far behind enemy lines.

Not that he was about to call them on it. In the circumstances, it was probably safer just to play along. The Battle of Tupelo had been fought back in the middle of July, its objective being to stop the Confederates destroying vital Union supply lines and potentially stalling General Sherman's advance on Atlanta.

'I hear it was a tough one,' he allowed.

'As you say,' agreed Clem. 'But not so tough that we couldn't've pressed it, iffen we'd been of a mind. Should've finished Nate Forrest right there an' then, my opinion. Would've, too, but it 'pears that Smith had other ideas — '

'Dammit!' hissed Harvey, interrupting his companion with a warning jab. 'You talk too much!'

'What did I say?'

'Enough so's we can't risk this here Cody passin' it on!'

'*What?*'

Harvey stabbed a finger at the boy. 'Who's to say he ain't really a Reb?

That he won't go straight back to the rest of his kind and tell 'em what you just told him?'

'I didn't tell him *anythin'!*'

But Harvey had made up his mind. 'Sorry, Cody, happen that *is* your name — but I reckon we' gonna have to shoot you now.'

Flat on his back in the middle of the glade, Will went cold. 'What? *Why?* I mean, I just said who I was, didn't I? That I'm on your side?'

'Sayin' it don't make it so,' countered Harvey.

'Now *listen*, fellers, you can't *do* this. I'm on important business for — '

' — Gen'ral Smith. Yeah, you said.'

'But if I don't carry out my orders — '

Clem, who had been giving the matter some thought, suddenly asked: 'You got any proof on you, Cody? To back up what you say, I mean?'

Before he could stop himself, Will snorted. '*Proof?* You ever seen a spy carryin' *proof?*'

8

'Ain't never seen a spy carryin' nothin',' said Clem.

'Truth be told,' added Harvey, 'we ain't never even seen a *spy*. But, fact is, it's you or us, young 'un. We're in enemy territory right now. We let you go on about your business, who's to say you won't turn us straight over to the Rebs?'

'Because I'm *not* a Reb! Hell, I want to avoid them Gray Backs as much as *you* do — probably more!'

Silence fell, broken only by the calls of sparrows and kittiwakes, returning to their nests after spooking during the ambush.

Clem took the tip of the bayonet from Will's throat and said to his companion: 'Be a sorry shame to shoot him, 'specially if'n he *is* one of us.'

He got up off the boy.

'I *am* one of you,' Will assured him earnestly, sitting up and checking his ribs to make sure nothing was cracked. 'I *swear* it.' Climbing to his feet, he gestured to the coiled guy-line rope

Harvey was carrying over one shoulder, then offered his hands, wrist over wrist. 'Tell you what. Why don't you just tie me up, and I promise I won't even *try* to get loose until after you've both long gone? I won't even tell anyone we ever met.'

Harvey and Clem exchanged a look.

At length Harvey said: 'Seems sound.'

So they tied Will up.

And just to make sure he kept his word, they also strung him upside-down from the nearest oak tree.

2

There was no call for that. There really wasn't. But at least he was still breathing. That was something, he guessed.

Still, his situation didn't look good. Clem and Harvey had tied his hands behind his back, Harvey in particular making sure the knots were as tight as ticks. Then, ignoring his protests, the two privates had tied his ankles and, throwing the free end of what remained of the guy-line over the stoutest bough of the nearest tree, had hauled him upside-down.

'No offense,' Harvey apologized as he tied some more solid knots around the bough. 'But you *might* be the enemy, no matter what you say to the contrary. We jus' got no way to know for sure, have we? Anyways, I daresay someone'll be along presently. They'll let you down — mebbe.'

Clem, meanwhile, took ownership of the fallen two-shot percussion pistol and hooked a thumb toward the plow horse, which was now grazing on a patch of grama grass a few yards away. Too late, Will realized that the theft of his horse had been their plan all along.

'We'll be takin' your mount, too,' said Clem. 'I know he don't look like much, but he's strong enough to carry two, I reckon, an' the sooner we get back to our own kind, the better we'll feel.'

'You're makin' a mistake,' said Will. 'Worse'n that, you might well make things a whole heap worse for the North.'

'That,' said Clem, 'is a chance we'll take. So long, Cody.'

And so saying, the two privates scrambled up onto the plow horse and rode away.

That had been twenty minutes earlier.

Now, with his head pounding fit to bust and his face flushed with blood, Will told himself that he had better find a way to free himself soon — or at very least turn himself right-side up again — or his goose would be well and truly cooked.

He struggled fruitlessly for a while longer, but only succeeded in chafing his wrists and straining back, belly and thigh muscles he didn't even know he had. Around him, the upside-down glade swung to and fro and round about, and the birds in the trees sung and twittered as if they hadn't a care in the world.

He twisted and turned some more, this time dislodging a small copper cylinder he'd been carrying in his shirt pocket — a collapsible spyglass telescope. The spyglass fell to the grass beneath him with a soft thud and he groaned, hoping he hadn't damaged the lens.

Then all further thought came to an abrupt halt as he realized he was being watched.

Swinging himself around, he saw a little girl of no more than seven, half-hidden in a row of butterfly bushes at the edge of the glade. She looked about as Southern as mint juleps in her blue gingham dress and copper ringlets. He had no idea how long she'd been standing there; he'd neither seen nor heard her approach.

As hard as it was to do so, Will forced himself to smile. He guessed that, upside-down it must look more like a grimace.

'H . . . Howdy,' he managed.

The girl stared at him through wide, lake-blue eyes.

'Sure be . . . obliged if you'd . . . untie me, missy . . .'

Staying right where she was, the girl said: 'Can't.'

'Wh — why, sure you can, child. Just . . . slip around . . . behind me an' . . . fiddle these here knots loose. I'll do the rest.'

Again the girl said: 'Can't.'

'Why not?'

''Cause you're a Yankee spy.'

'A what, now?' He forced a laugh.

'Oh, I get it. You . . . must've heard me talkin' to them other fellers. The ones that tied me up.'

She nodded, her expression very grave.

'Hidin' in them there . . . bushes, was you?' he asked, feeling the blood pulsing even stronger in his temples.

Again the girl nodded.

'Well,' Will breathed, 'I can see how you're . . . confused . . . 'bout me bein' a Yankee spy 'n' all.'

'Mean you ain't?'

''Course not, child. Had to . . . tell them Bluebellies that, though . . . else they'd've skewered me.'

The girl looked skeptical.

'I mean, do I . . . look like a spy to you?'

She shrugged.

'Well, I don't,' he assured her. 'Take my word for it, an' — '

The girl turned and started to walk away.

'*Hey!* Where y'all goin'? Hey, wait up, missy!'

It was on the tip of his tongue to promise her everything from Necco Wafers to a brand new wind-up doll if only she'd help him down, but it seemed her mind was made up. This was something beyond her young grasp. It was something that grown-ups were better suited to figure out.

He swore under his breath.

Then she was gone, and he was all alone.

Damn!

General A. J. Smith, more recently promoted to Lieutenant Colonel, hadn't needed to spell it out to him during their interview, of course, but he had anyway.

They tell me you're a scout of some talent despite your tender years, Private Cody. Right now I need a man of such skill. But what I have in mind calls for my man to go behind enemy lines dressed as a civilian. You know what that means, of course?

Of course he did. If he was caught out of uniform, he'd be shot as a spy.

But convinced that he *wouldn't* be caught, he'd nodded and said: 'What do you want me to do, sir?'

He'd received his orders, and dressed as a seemingly innocent farm boy had successfully crossed into enemy territory . . . but now it looked as if his mission was over before he'd even had a chance to start it.

Damn it, damn it, damn it — !

The rustle of brush being shoved aside, followed by the brisk approach of heavy boots, brought him back to the present. Once again he used his body like a pendulum to turn himself around just as a tall, lean man in Confederate gray came striding into the clearing with the girl at his side.

Will thought: *Aw . . . shoot.*

The man's uniform told its own story. The woolen frock coat was well tailored, each of its fourteen brass buttons polished to a high gleam. Here was a dandy, then, who dressed to impress, for frock coats were not standard issue in the Confederate

Army. The buff-colored cuffs and collar suggested that the newcomer was more of an administrator than a fighter — in which case Will could only hope that the long, gently curved saber in the metal scabbard hanging at his side was merely for show. The three bars the man wore on each shoulder signified his rank — that of captain.

''Morning, sir,' said Will. 'Cody's my name. Reckon the girl told you what happened, so — '

'She says you're a Yankee spy, son,' interrupted the officer.

Trying his best to look scandalized by the suggestion, Will said in a rush: 'Oh, God Almighty, *no*, sir. Why, I was born on a farm just a few miles east of Springfield . . . Missouri, that is. You must've heard of it — '

'Hold it, son,' said the officer. As near as Will could see from upside-down, he was a sharp-featured but nonetheless handsome man in his mid-twenties, with long, curly ash-brown hair and an impressive, well-clipped handlebar mustache.

Addressing the girl, he said gently: 'Run on home, child. Tell your Pa I'll be along soon as I've finished here.'

Will swallowed — no mean feat when you're strung upside down. But there was something about the phrase, some-thing downright *ominous*, that he didn't like.

As if to confirm his suspicions, the officer waited until the girl had gone and then drew his saber. As Will watched, he used the weapon to slice the air with a series of short, vicious swipes.

'Now, h-hold *up*, captain! You gotta believe me! I ain't no Yankee spy, and that's the truth — '

'Don't lie, son,' said the officer, coming closer. 'You don't want to meet your Maker spilling untruths, now, do you?'

'But I — '

The saber slashed through the air and Will flinched, closed his eyes, clenched his teeth and fell headfirst to the ground, landing hard on his spyglass.

It took him a moment to understand

that the blow had not been aimed at him, but at the rope around his ankles. And even as he realized that — wonder of wonders — his head was still attached to his shoulders, the Confederate officer began to laugh.

He stared up at the man, seeing him right-side up for the first time, and started to demand what in hell was so damn' funny.

Then he froze.

There was something familiar about the officer that he hadn't recognized upside-down.

He *knew* this man.

He thought: *I'll be damned.*

It was his old friend, James Butler 'Wild Bill' Hickok.

3

Will angrily croaked: 'Bill . . . '

But Hickok only laughed harder as he returned his saber to its scabbard. He then employed a trembling falsetto to mimic the youngster: ''Oh, God Almighty, no, sir . . . Why, I was born on a farm just a few miles east of Springfield . . . Missouri, that is.''

Will reddened but said no more.

Let Hickok have his moment. God knows, he owed Wild Bill that and more. Bill was a legend, even then. Grizzly killer, teamster, gambler, scout, gunfighter, wagon master, policeman — sometimes Will felt there was nothing this tall, lean, likeable man couldn't tackle, conquer and make look easy as pie.

He and Hickok had met when Will was just a twelve year-old kid in the employ of the freight company Russell,

Majors & Waddell, and Hickok had been a scout on the same payroll. They'd bonded tight as brothers right from the start . . . and so now Will waited as patiently as he could until Hickok's mirth dried up and he finally knelt beside Will and cut the ropes binding his wrists and ankles.

As Will rubbed life back into his limbs and retrieved his spyglass, Hickok took a canteen off the back of his belt and passed it over. Water, Will decided, had never tasted so good.

'Hell's fire, Will,' Hickok said, flopping down on the grass beside his young friend, 'I still don't know which way up you looks best. Them roses in your cheeks sure are fetchin' . . .'

'You know,' said Will, glaring at Hickock, 'you 'n' Jim Bridger got the same sense of humor . . . which is no damn sense of humor at all!'

'Well, where's the sense in sheddin' tears, boy? You're a long time dead. Fella might as well have some fun while he can.'

'I don't see the fun to be had from another man's misfortune,'Will grumbled. 'But I got to say, partner, it's good to see you.'

Hickok finally sobered. 'What in hell you doin' way out here, anyway — and in them duds?'

'I was about to ask you the same thing.'

Hickok lowered his voice. 'I'm spyin' for General McNeil,' he said.

Will looked surprised. 'You mean you're still with the army? I thought you was workin' as some kind of lawman for the provost marshal in Springfield?'

'Lot of folks think that,' allowed Hickok. 'It's what I *want* 'em to think.'

'McNeil,' Will repeated thoughtfully. 'I've carried dispatches for him myself in the past. But right now, I got bigger fish to fry.'

'How so?'

'There's talk of a large mounted force comin' up out from Arkansas under the command of Sterling Price.'

'I know. It was me first passed the

word along to higher headquarters.'

'Then you also know it looks like he's plannin' to invade Missouri,' Will added.

Hickock grunted in acknowledgement. It was common knowledge that if Price captured St Louis and reclaimed Missouri for the Confederacy, it would have a devastating effect on Union morale. Furthermore, if his success encouraged Union sympathizers to defect to the Confederate cause . . . well, such factors could potentially spell defeat for Lincoln in the November elections, and put a Confederate president in the White House.

As he retrieved his old palm-leaf hat, Will explained that he'd been sent to confirm the rumors, and if possible get an accurate idea of the enemy's true strength. Only then could the deployment of vast numbers of Union troops from Tennessee, Kansas and Missouri itself be justified.

Hickok indicated north with a jerk of his chin. 'Well, Price is hereabouts, right enough, just across the line there in Arkansas, as you say. As to his strength, I ain't had a chance to ghost on over and take a look yet. But I tell you what. If you want to come on back to the girl's house, I'll borrow you a horse, give you a spare gun an' tell you where you can find him.'

'Thanks.'

As Hickok led the way around one vast cornfield after another, he told Will that he'd managed to finagle himself a position on the staff of General Kirby Smith. It was there, whilst masquerading as 'Captain Arnold Buller' that he'd first heard news of Price's recently-assembled 'Army of Missouri'. The little girl's father, he said, was a Union sympathizer and go-between who had passed the information along on his behalf.

'I usually call in on him once or twice a week,' Hickok finished. 'Partly for appearances' sake, partly because his wife's a damn' fine cook, and I've no great liking for the slops the Gray Backs call food. So it was your good fortune I was around to save your sorry hide today, young Will. Be a damned shame to see a feller like you cut off in his prime.'

Though Will refrained from comment, he shook his head in wonder. Hickok had always seen something in him — some kind of raw energy or potential — that Will himself had been completely unaware of. Of course, Hickok hadn't called it that. 'Spit an' grit,' was how he'd described it. Will had no idea whether or not he'd ever justify Hickok's faith in him, but there was no denying that he'd been right when he talked about good fortune: if that little girl had fetched anyone other than Hickok back to the glade, Will's luck would have run out — for good.

Fifteen minutes later they came to a sorry-looking log and mud-chinked cabin that sat behind a sagging porch. Here Hickok introduced Will to his friend, John Prentiss, Prentiss's wife Heather and the little girl, whose name was Amy. Prentiss himself turned out to be a sad-faced man of about thirty, who was missing his right arm. The little girl got her copper coloring from him.

Mrs. Prentiss invited Will to stay for the midday meal — collard beans and cornbread — but hungry though he was, he was also anxious to push on and carry out his mission.

'What's your hurry, Will?' asked Hickok when he declined the invitation.

'I just figure — '

' — to stroll right on into Price's camp an' get yourself killed?'

Will grimaced. 'Thanks for the vote of confidence.'

'Oh, far be it from me to *undermine* you, young William. I jus' wonder when you'll learn is all.'

'Learn what?'

'That the spy's best friend is — '

' — darkness,' Will finished automatically.

He realized then what he should have known all along — that he stood more chance of approaching Price's cantonment under cover of night, and could use the hours until dusk to rest up here in relative safety and be fresh for his scout. That being the case, he offered Mrs. Prentiss his warmest smile and said: 'Ma'am, if you'll allow me to change my mind, I reckon I'd be proud to take food with you after all.'

And that's exactly what he did.

When he and Hickok finally pulled out a little before sunset, Will had a fresh mount under him and a seven-shot Moore's belt revolver to replace the pistol Clem Butterfield had taken.

'You don't have to guide me all the way, you know,' Will said as the Prentiss cabin fell behind them. 'All I need are directions.'

'That's what I like about you, Will,' Hickok replied, matching Will's cautious undertone. 'You think you can do it all — and one of these days, my ears for a heeltap if you don't.'

'But not tonight?'

'You're a good student, Will,' Hickok went on. 'Best I ever saw. But even *you* don't know everything yet. So jus' quit your yammer an' keep your eyes peeled. For all his faults, that Price is a wily old cuss, so from now on we move nice 'n' quiet.'

They crossed the Mississippi-Arkansas line a little after one in the morning. A narrow slice of moon provided the only illumination. The night was humid and Will found himself sweating. At length Hickok drew rein on the edge of yet another cornfield and thumbed at an ink-black line of timber, mostly oak and hickory, about half a mile north.

'You'll find Price's camp the other side of them trees,' he said.

Will glanced at him. The moonlight made it look as his profile was etched in chalk. 'Thanks, Bill.'

' 'Nada. Just do your job, get all the information General Smith needs — and then get your butt back out in one piece.'

'I'll do that.'

He reached out and the two friends shook hands. No further words passed between them. Hickok simply turned his mount and started walking it back south until man and beast were both lost in shadow.

After Hickok was gone Will felt curiously alone. Neither did the cornfield off to his left, with its distinctive smell of honey, flower-scent and good, rich dirt, do anything to make him feel any better. It only woke memories — painful ones — that he'd sooner not disturb.

Then he squared his shoulders. This was no time to think about the past. He dismounted and tethered his horse in a scraggy thicket on the far side of the rutted track that bordered the cornfield. Then, checking that he had his spyglass, a scrap of paper and a stub of pencil, he set off toward the distant trees, moving as stealthily as he could.

4

It was as well that he did, because Price had pickets out — a lot of them. But to Will's mind they seemed a careless bunch and he found himself frowning, for given Price's reputation as a fire-eater, he'd have expected better.

As it was, he caught the scent of tobacco on the night air long before the first picket came into sight and immediately went to ground. A few moments later, through a screen of brush, he watched two sorry-looking men meet up fifty feet ahead of him, one of them smoking a pipe, the other a hand-rolled cigarette. Will identified their short-barreled weapons as antiquated musketoons. Their uniforms were in poor shape too, and they appeared to be missing most of their equipment — canteens, cartridge boxes —

Will could hardly credit it, but these

two weren't even wearing boots!

The pickets exchanged a few words and moved on. Even barefoot, they made enough noise to wake a rock. They were amateurs, he realized, not professional soldiers at all.

He wondered if all of Price's men were as poorly trained and equipped, but doubted it. More likely, Price had been forced to take on recaptured deserters and other shady specimens, just to make up the numbers of his invading force.

Crouching low and choosing every step with care, Will headed for the far side of the trees. The stand of timber gradually thinned until it opened out onto a broad valley that Price had chosen as his cantonment. The sickle moon, plus the light cast by the odd campfire here and there, showed him row upon row of tents. They were all kinds: dog-, Sibley, A-frame and wall tents. This bivouac area seemed to go on forever, and covered most of the valley.

With infinite caution Will began to circle the location, stopping every now and then to note down the number of wagons, the state of their supplies (which was meager), the condition of the Confederate cavvy (mostly old hay-chompers) and the number of artillery pieces with them. There were fourteen in all — six twelve-pounder Howitzers, six ten-pounder Parrott rifles and a pair of old twelve-pounder Napoleons.

Several times throughout the night he had to seek cover as a ragged Gray Back broke his rest to visit the latrine, or a picket appeared out of the darkness, whistling softly or humming under his breath. It was demanding work, and Will soon began to feel the strain. He'd never undertaken a scout of this size or importance before, and to be in the presence of so many Confederate troops all at once

A new thought occurred to him. How many were there, anyway? That was something else General Smith needed to know. That they were poorly outfitted had quickly become obvious to him. But even a poorly outfitted army could win the day with sufficient numbers.

He checked the sky and was startled to find that dawn was little more than an hour away. He had no idea how time had passed so quickly. Turning his attention back to the camp, he tried to estimate numbers, but it was impossible to do so with any accuracy.

Then an idea occurred to him and he returned the way he'd come. Already the camp was beginning to stir; men were crawling out of their dog tents, relieving themselves or stirring small fires to life and boiling up breakfasts of what smelled like polk and potato tops, kurlip weed and thistles.

Although time was against him, he knew better than to hurry. If just one Gray Back should spot him and raise the alarm, he was finished. So he forced himself to move at the same cautious pace he'd used on his first circuit of the camp, until at length he reached the trees again.

He felt spent and was damp with sweat. Nevertheless, he quickly selected and climbed a gnarled hickory, using all the experience gained in childhood to find one foot- and hand-hold after another. At one point a blackbird exploded from the tangle of branches directly above him and he froze. Only when no one raised the alarm did he release a breath and continue climbing.

About fifteen feet up he finally spotted a thick bough that was ideal for his purpose. Stretching out on his stomach and clamping his knees around the limb, he began to inspect the camp through his spyglass.

For the first time, the spyglass, plus his greater elevation, enabled him to see the camp almost in its entirety. Working swiftly now, he calculated the number of tents in a given block and then multiplied it by the number of blocks he could see from his vantage point. That gave him a rough but accurate-enough number of tents. Assuming two men to a tent —

For a few seconds he scribbled on his scrap of paper and then paused.

Unless he was well wide of the mark, the Army of Missouri was about twelve thousand strong.

Tucking the paper and pencil away, he took up the spyglass again and was just about to give the camp one final survey when —

'*Hey, you!*'

Will jerked in surprise and almost fell from the bough.

'What'n the hell you doin' up there, kid?'

Taking the telescope from his eye, Will looked down at the speaker, who was just visible in the lifting gloom. Although he'd called Will a kid, they were actually about the same age. And the youngster who was pointing a rifle up at him was wearing just enough of a uniform — képi, plain gray trousers over a pair of old, worn-leather brogans, and a rolled blanket tied over the shoulder of his butternut shirt — to reveal that he was one of the pickets

Will had worked so hard to avoid.

Heart hammering, Will played up to his guileless farm-boy appearance. 'Why, nothin', sir! Jus' ... I was curious about all this here activity an' snuck up to get a better look at all them soldier-boys. Right purty sight, sir. Makes me want to up an' join 'em.'

The picket scratched his head and looked skeptical. Will didn't blame him. His performance was hardly convincing. The picket growled: 'Get on down here an' tell your lies to Sergeant Morris.'

'Yessir,' Will said eagerly, 'but it's the God's honest truth, I swear it.'

He shifted position slightly, apparently searching for the safest way to descend from his perch. Then, in a sudden burst of action, he flung the spyglass down at his captor.

The spyglass tumbled end over end, spilling new-day sunshine off its curved copper surface, and hit the picket square in the face.

Startled, he gasped with pain and

took a clumsy backward step, dropping his rifle in order to clutch at his newly broken nose.

Will didn't give the rebel any chance to recover. He quickly leaped down from the branch, absorbing of the twelve or more feet by landing on bent knees. He tumbled sideways, recovered instantly and hurled himself at his opponent. Momentum carried them up against the bole of the tree: the rebel guard wheezed as Will crushed him against its shaggy bark.

The fear of being shot as a spy kept Will moving. He grabbed the guard by one shoulder and used his other hand to smash him in the face. Cartilage crunched again as he punched the picket twice in succession and then twice more. The boy fell like a puddle at his feet.

Grabbing up his fallen palm leaf hat and spyglass, Will scanned his surroundings again. His breathing was harsh. But as near as he could tell, the alarm still hadn't been raised. Relieved, he turned and started trotting back through the trees the way he'd come.

'*Hey — you there!*'

The yell echoed hollowly through the air. With a curse Will pivoted, saw another equally sorry-looking picket fifty yards away, now bringing a Lorenz rifle to one shoulder. He broke into a run, bracing himself for the shot he knew must come.

It didn't disappoint. There was a snap of sound, a whine of lead, a pulpy smack as the Minié ball thudded into a tree he'd just passed.

Will kept running. Now all that existed was the woods ahead, the hiss and saw of his labored breathing, the crush and crack of leaf and twig as his legs powered him on.

Shouting erupted behind him. He couldn't distinguish the words, but they were easy enough to guess.

What's going on?

Over there — someone spyin' on the camp!

Get 'im!

Another shot tore through the air. Will swore he felt the wind of the ball as it passed him. He started zigging and zagging to make a harder target of himself, but already his lungs were burning and he could hear sounds of pursuit as other pickets came racing to the scene.

Without warning a fuzzy-bearded Confederate appeared in his path and fired his musketoon from the hip. The hasty shot went wide. Giving him no chance to improve his aim, Will snatched at the weapon's barrel and yanked it from the rebel's grasp. Even as the picket clawed for the Colt Dragoon tucked behind his belt, Will swung the musketoon like a club. The stock slammed into the side of the Confederate's head and he collapsed, squirting blood from both ears.

Another volley crashed through the woods. Will threw himself flat, slithered along on his belly into a shallow depression and pulled the belt revolver Hickok had given him. Turning, he came up over the lip of the depression and thumbed off three fast shots. Out there someone yelled a startled curse and then it went quiet.

Will turned again, launched himself up and continued running. If he could just make it to his horse he stood a chance of getting away, but his legs were still stiff from having spent so long in the tree and the going was hard.

Another Confederate appeared twenty yards in front of him. Instinctively he raised the revolver and fired. The soldier went over backwards, leaving a red mist in the air to mark his passing.

Will leaped over the body and kept going. More gunshots popped behind him. But there, up ahead, the trees began to thin and the cornfield showed bright yellow in the rising sun.

Another crack of sound; another explosion of bark that sprayed him with sap and splinters.

He struggled on, everything a blur, and finally burst out of the trees and into the new day's warmth. Somehow he found the strength to continue running, the breath rasping in his ears all but drowning the baying yells of his pursuers.

He dodged into the cornfield. With the stalks already standing fifteen feet high, it quickly swallowed him whole. Yet again it stirred memories in him, memories of his childhood, of his father, of trouble and eventual death. Once more he dismissed them, shoved the pistol behind his belt and began to bat and swipe his way between the rows like a man swimming.

Taking care to avoid exposed roots, he cut a diagonal path toward the thicket in which he'd tied his horse. Behind him, he heard sounds of pursuit. It told him that his pursuers were slowly but surely gaining on him.

For some indeterminate time it was just bat and swipe, bat and swipe as he worked his way ever south and east. Then, at last, he stumbled out of the field and onto the rutted track that ran alongside it. He looked to right and left, spotted the thicket and hurried toward it.

The dozing horse nickered a greeting as Will came into sight. Untying the animal, he swung astride, turned its big head and started south at a run.

He thought: *I'm gonna make it, I'm actually gonna* —

Then a gunshot shattered the morning air and beneath him the horse staggered and broke stride. Cursing, Will hipped around and saw the three Confederate pickets who'd been pursuing him come to an untidy halt on the track beside the cornfield.

One of them raised his rifle and another shot rang out. This time the horse went down, forelegs first, and the rebels cheered and started running again, confident now that they would catch their man.

With neither saddle nor stirrup to halt his forward momentum, Will sailed over the dying horse's head and landed hard against the ground. The impact knocked all the wind out of him and he took a savage rap to the head.

No . . . no . . .

With the world spinning around him, he tried to rise but only succeeded in falling sideways. He had no better luck trying to draw the belt revolver in order to defend himself from his approaching enemies.

He thought about the information he'd gathered and how it would never now get back to General Smith, and vaguely tried to use the anger and despair in him to stave off unconsciousness — or worse.

Blood thundered in his ears, and the ground under him began to shake — or was that just him, trembling harder than ever as he continued to fight his losing battle with darkness?

The thunder grew, suddenly resolving itself into the pound of horse hooves, coming on hard. And then —

A sudden flurry of shots sounded directly overhead. Eyes closed, already sinking into oblivion, he still flinched at the sound.

His world went silent then but for the occasional stamp of a horse's hooves, the sound of a man dismounting nearby. As if from a long way off he felt strong arms scoop him up and carry him back to the waiting horse. He distantly heard a voice he recognized as Bill Hickok's, saying: 'That's the second time in less than a day I've pulled your fat from the fire, Will. Still reckon you know everything?'

Will made no reply. He was dead to the world.

The world went silent then but Twelve
wondered ... stamp of a horse's hooves,
the sound of a man ... whispering
nearby. As if from a long way off ... he
could ... scoop ... up and carry
him back to the waiting horse. He
... heard ... he recognised as
... saw ... But the sound
... less than a day we pulled your
... the fog. Will ... Still reckon you
... soon enough.

With ... no reply, Twelve was dead to
the world ...

Part Two — Avenger

5

Hickok delivered Will — and Will's notes on the enemy's strength — to the camp of General A. J. Smith twenty-four hours later. Will, still unconscious, was taken straight to the field hospital.

'He gonna pull through, doc?' Hickok asked when the army surgeon finished examining the boy.

The army surgeon, a tired-looking, balding man of middle age, pondered the question for a moment and then nodded. 'I believe so, yes.'

'It's just that . . . well, he hasn't come round yet. I'd have thought by now — '

'Don't let that worry you, Hickok. The body often shuts itself down while it heals. When you've seen as many wounded men as I have, you almost come to expect it.'

The surgeon looked down at the boy on the narrow canvas cot before him. A

49

bump the size of a woman's fist still stood proud on Will's pale temple.

'He's young, he's strong. I'd put good money on him regaining consciousness any time now and showing few if any ill effects. Hell, if a man can be shot in the forehead and live to tell the tale, you can bet your boy there will be just fine.'

Hickok eyed the surgeon sidelong. 'Are you joshin' me, doc? A man shot in the forehead lived to tell about it?'

'Not only did he live to tell about it,' the surgeon remarked cheerfully, 'he's still got the hole right between his eyes to prove it. And before you call me a liar, I can tell you I've seen him myself, large as life and twice as chipper!'

As the surgeon strode off to deal with his other patients, Hickok clapped his hat on and looked at Will. To see the normally vital boy so lifeless made him wince. 'Some of us still got a war to fight, Will,' he said in an undertone. 'So I got to be pushin' along. You, ah . . . you just get better, all right?'

Will gave no indication that he had heard the words.

Deep inside his brain, however, he knew that he'd been injured somehow. Well . . . that had been bound to happen sooner or later. He'd already packed in plenty of living as it was: and he'd always known that a boy who lived life the way he had was never going to make old bones.

Will's first exposure to violence had come when he was just nine years old.

As the family's spring wagon crested the rise and rattled on down into the grass-rich Kansas valley below, his father, Isaac, spotted a group of hard-faced men loitering outside Riveley's Trading Post and knew immediately that they meant trouble.

The post itself had never been much — a sprawling, single-story clapboard and cedar-shake affair flanked by a corral, an outhouse, a barn and a couple of storage sheds. But in such a vast and under-populated land it served as a regular meeting place for those who lived within its reach.

Isaac had come in that day to collect the money Riveley owed him for the hay and wood he'd supplied to the storekeeper. Now, knowing there could be no avoiding the confrontation to come, he cursed his bad timing.

On the seat beside him, young Will looked up from Turk, the chocolate-colored hound sitting across his lap, and seeing the crowd, asked: 'What's goin' on, pa?'

'Beats me,' Isaac lied. He was a lean, weathered man in his mid-forties, whose gentle voice still betrayed its Canadian origins. The boy favored him in build and coloring, and though time had tempered Isaac's once impulsive, adventurous nature, the boy had inherited that, too.

Isaac Cody, his wife Mary Ann and their five children had arrived in Kansas two years earlier, at a time when the territory was just opening up to settlers. With an eye to the future, Isaac had staked a claim that encompassed part of the Great Salt Lake trail, and as a consequence young Will's life had been one of continual discovery.

First, he'd made new friends with the local Kickapoo children, and even learned their language, as well as some of their more complex 'whistle speech.' Then there was the regular passage of Russell, Majors & Waddell freight wagons, carrying supplies to the ever-increasing number of forts dotting the plains. Over time, Will had become friendly with all the rough-and-ready wagon-masters, bull-whackers and cavayard drivers who followed the trains with herds of extra oxen.

But he was too young to know anything about the trouble that had been brewing in the territory for a while now — trouble that threatened to erupt into full-scale war as Kansas made plans to enter the Union as its thirty-fourth state.

The question of slavery had split the territory between the 'Free Staters', who wanted to see its abolition, and the 'Border Ruffians', who were keen to continue what they saw as an acceptable tradition.

Because Isaac never talked politics, folks who knew him had naturally assumed that he agreed with the pro-slavery views of his brother Elijah, who owned and ran a general store in Weston, just across the Kansas line in Missouri.

Isaac had never bothered to correct them. At the time it had seemed the best way to avoid making enemies when there was no need.

But he'd always known that one day the truth would come out: and sure enough, when it was discovered that he had once been a Free Soil man (so-named for a short-lived political party that opposed slavery in the western territories), it had become clear where his allegiance really lay.

From that day on, he hadn't so much made enemies as simply lost friends.

Now, as he drew his spring wagon to a halt beside those of the other men there, all heads turned to watch his arrival. Their expressions were almost uniformly hostile.

Swallowing, Will said softly: 'Shoulda

let me bring the rifle, Pa.'

'A man don't bear arms against his neighbors, Will,' Isaac reminded him. 'Come on, let's just tend to our business an' then get on back to the —'

It was then that he spotted his brother among the crowd. Elijah was considered an important man in those parts, and rightly so. He was a large exporter of hemp as well as a general trader — and slave-owner.

As their eyes met, Elijah gave his head an urgent little tilt, his message clear.

Get out of here while you still can.

But that was the hell of it. Isaac *was* here now, and he couldn't just turn around and go on home without losing what little face he still had left. Like it or not, he had to see this business through.

Turk leapt from the wagon and Isaac and Cody followed him down. Isaac had an uneasy suspicion that most of the men in attendance had been drinking. Their flushed faces and belligerent manner seemed to confirm it.

Up until their arrival, the assembly had been listening to a large, surly man standing on an upturned dry goods box beneath the peeling sign that read RIVELEY'S TRADING POST — M. PIERCE RIVELEY, PROP. Though tall, he was slightly stooped, as if weighed down by his own great size. His name was Charles Dunn, and one way or another he and Isaac had never seen eye to eye on anything.

Now Dunn raised his massive, work-hardened hands for silence, and got it at once. Taking a sheet of paper from the pocket of his oft-repaired box jacket, he raised his slow, rumbling voice and read:

'The first provision added to the Salt Creek Valley Resolution is as follows: 'That we recognize the institution of slavery as always existin' in this Territory, and recommend that slave-holders introduce their property as soon as possible.''

There was a buzz of agreement from the onlookers.

'Second,' Dunn continued ponderously: ' "That we afford no protection to Abolitionists as settlers of Kansas Territory." '

As his audience roared its approval, Dunn turned to Isaac, who with Will was about to enter the store. 'You hear that, Cody?' he called.

The cheering tapered off. Suddenly, it went stone quiet.

Pausing, Isaac looked at Dunn. 'I heard it,' he replied mildly.

'An' that's all you got to say about it?'

'Would *anything* I said make any difference?'

Before Dunn could respond, a near neighbor, Abel Floodwater, said: 'Seems only right you should declare yourself, Cody!'

'Got no opinion, either way,' Isaac replied.

'That's a lie an' you know it!'

'Well, what else would you expect from a damn' Abolitionist?' Dunn demanded of the crowd.

That inspired another ugly murmuring.

Isaac pushed Will toward the trading post. 'Get along inside, boy.'

'But, Pa — '

'Don't argue with me, son.'

Reluctantly, Will did as he was told. But no sooner had he disappeared through the doorway than he ran to the nearest tarpaper window, compelled to watch whatever happened next.

Dunn jumped down off his box and lumbered toward Isaac. The crowd parted before him. He was a jowly man of about thirty, with big, open pores and a shock of greasy, pure-black hair. Beneath his jacket, Dunn's nankeen shirt and California pants struggled to accommodate his bulk.

He planted himself directly in front of Isaac, dwarfing him but — to his annoyance — not intimidating him. He stabbed an accusing finger in Isaac's face and rasped: 'We want an answer, Cody. You for or agin slavery?'

'Slavery's wrong,' Isaac replied. 'It should be stopped.'

'See?' said Dunn, swinging back to his audience. 'What'd I tell you? Man's nothin' but a pig-swillin' Abolitionist!'

'I'm not an Abolitionist,' Isaac responded, raising his voice to be heard over the crowd's angry response, 'and I never have been. What I'm opposed to is extendin' slavery beyond the states it's in right now. Leave it there — and keep it out of Kansas.'

'Then you're sayin' we're all wrong?' goaded Dunn.

'I'm saying you're entitled to your opinion, just as I am.'

'But you don't agree with us,' Dunn pressed.

'That's not a crime, is it?'

'Maybe not,' said Dunn. 'But if you're not *with* us, Cody, you're *agin* us . . . and that makes you a man we don't want in these parts. Right, boys?'

Primed for just this moment, the crowd — Elijah being the only exception — surged forward and Isaac swiftly vanished from sight.

Inside the store, Riveley was halfway up a rolling ladder stocking shelves with his back to the door. It seemed impossible to Will that he couldn't hear the sounds of the mob outside. But then, he was too young to fully understand the desire some men have just not to get involved.

'Mr. Riveley!' he called, raising his voice above Turk's furious barking, 'you gotta stop 'em! They're hurtin' Pa!'

Up on his ladder, Riveley went on stocking shelves, pretending he hadn't heard the boy, and despising himself for it.

'Please, Mr. Riveley . . . if you don't stop 'em, they're gonna *kill* him!'

Still Riveley stacked his shelves.

Outside, meanwhile, Isaac had pulled himself free of his tormentors. Someone had punched him and his left eye was already swelling shut. There was blood on his teeth, too: he could taste it. And that's what this crowd wanted, now: it was clear in every flushed expression.

They wanted blood.

Dunn came closer, his big fists slowly clenching, and in the circumstances Isaac did the only thing he could — he lashed out with a right jab that caught Dunn square on the jaw.

The blow sent Dunn reeling back into his cohorts. They caught him and shoved him forward again before he could fall. Furious now, Dunn hurled himself at Isaac. His first flailing blow connected and Isaac fell against the wagon with his ears ringing. Other hands grabbed his arms then and dragged him away from the vehicle. Isaac distantly heard Charles Dunn yell: 'Somebody get a whip!'

Isaac shook his head, partly to clear it, partly to stop any of his tormentors from carrying out the order. 'No!' he cried, spitting blood. 'Listen to me! Hell, listen to *yourselves!*'

He moved quickly then, once again tore his arms from the men holding them and tried to make a break for it. But Dunn had been expecting as much.

As he went to block Isaac's path, Isaac dodged to one side and tried to slip around him. Then, even as his son watched through the store window, Isaac stiffened abruptly and his face froze in an expression of agony.

He fell forward. It was then Will saw blood on the back of his father's shirt: blood that was spreading fast.

Horrified, Will kept his eyes glued to the window and now saw a Bowie knife protruded from his father's blood-soaked back.

'Pa! *Pa!*'

Will burst out onto the porch, leapt down into the dirt and fought his way through the throng. There was no sound now; just an awful hush punctured by his own shuddery breathing. Then Will fought his way through the last of them — only to see Dunn, already kneeling beside Isaac, yank the knife from the wound and pocket it.

The rest of the men had seen it too. Sobered by the brutality of what they'd just witnessed, and wanting to distance themselves from it, they began to back away.

Riveley, hearing their subdued murmuring, descended from his ladder and came as far as his doorway.

Will kneeled beside his father and gently turned him onto his side. Isaac looked up at him, eyes mirroring his pain. His labored, indrawn breath made a sibilant hiss. Every muscle in him bunched up at once, and Will clutched one of his hands.

'Pa! Oh Lordy, Pa, what've they *done* to you?'

Isaac looked at him as if he were a stranger. Will had never seen that look before and it scared him to his core. Then Isaac said softly: 'Get me home, son.'

'Sure, Pa . . . sure . . . '

At last Elijah came forward and knelt beside them. He looked at the wound and he too made a hissing sound.

'Is it bad?' Will demanded.

'He's been cut through the kidneys, near as I can tell,' Elijah replied shakily.

Will felt tears burn his cheeks. 'It was that feller Dunn who did it!'

'I know,' Elijah said grimly. Dunn actually worked for him — *had* done, anyway. After this he was out of a job and likely to face a lengthy prison sentence at the very least. Elijah looked around, but only confirmed what he'd already guessed — that Dunn, knowing as much, had made his getaway. 'Let's get your pa into the wagon,' he said.

Together, Will and Elijah carried Isaac to the wagon. Shock had set in and Isaac was a dead weight. The mob — though it could hardly be called such now — watched in silence.

Riveley, feeling guilty for refusing to get involved, now emerged from his store and offered to help.

At the sound of his voice Will whirled and glared at him.

The fury in his eyes — the eyes of a boy now turned man — stopped Riveley.

'You didn't help my pa when he needed it,' Will said bitterly. 'So you can be damn' sure we don't need you now!'

Riveley's mouth worked awkwardly for a moment, but no words came out.

Not that Will was interested in hearing them, anyway. Turning away he said softly: 'C'mon, Uncle Lije. Let's get pa home.'

6

As Riveley's store fell behind them, reaction set in and Will began to tremble. He shook almost constantly as he kept the wagon headed for home and one thought repeating itself like a litany in his jumbled mind: *Don't die, Pa. Please don't die.*

In back, his uncle spent most of the journey fighting to staunch the flow of blood from Isaac's damaged kidney.

When the Cody cabin finally came into sight just beyond the cornfield that faced it, Turk leapt down from the wagon and ran on ahead, making a strange, barking howl as he went. Alerted by the sound Will's mother, Mary Ann, came running out in a rustle of calico, his fourteen year-old sister Julia, hurrying behind her.

Seeing Will alone on the high seat, and Elijah in back, Mary Ann realized that something was wrong and rushed to the tailgate as the wagon braked in the middle of the yard. She recoiled when she saw Isaac in the wagon bed, sprawled on a blood-spattered blanket.

A small, strong woman with auburn hair worn tight in a bun, she turned pale and one fist moved to her mouth. 'Oh Lordy,' she sobbed. 'What's happened?'

'Charles Dunn stabbed him!' said Will, jumping down from the wagon.

His mother shook her head as if unable to comprehend the news. '*What?* Why — ?'

Elijah gathered his brother up in his arms and climbed down from the bed. 'Why do you think?' he demanded irritably. 'Because he's Free State.'

In the comfortable parlor, the rest of Will's family — sisters Eliza, nine, Helen, seven, May, four and two year-old brother Charles — watched nervously as Elijah carried Isaac upstairs to the main bed-room. Isaac's face was pale as chalk and as if trapped in a nightmare, he moved his lips constantly, though the words he muttered were unintelligible.

As Mary Ann followed her tall, underfed-looking brother-in-law into the bedroom, she started to think about how they must deal with what had happened.

'I've about stopped the bleedin',' said Elijah, setting Isaac down on the bed and trying to make him as comfortable. 'Now it's up to the Lord whether he lives or not.'

Mary Ann nodded, mind racing, and turned to Julia, who was weeping hysterically. 'Girl, stop your crying! Boil up some salt water and fetch me some clean cloths! We need to wash that wound before we stitch it! Will — go fetch my sewing box and . . . and that bottle of grain alcohol in the dresser. And then . . . then . . . '

Her voice trailed off and she looked at Elijah, suddenly helpless.

As if sensing her distress, Turk began to howl out in the yard.

'Then,' finished Elijah, his voice close to a whisper, 'we pray.'

Somehow Isaac survived the rest of the day and Mary Ann watched over him through the night, bathing his forehead with cold water until, shortly after midnight, he turned feverish. Will, who had refused to go to bed but curled up in a corner of his parents' bedroom to sleep, waked to the sound of his father thrashing around. Together mother and son held Isaac as still as they could until, exhausted, he fell quiet again.

Will gazed at his mother. In the light of a turned-low lantern she looked worn out and the locks of her hair, having come unclipped, hung limply around her face. The only sound in the room came from the soft ticking of a cheap shelf clock.

Will reached out and grasped her hand. 'Don't worry, Ma,' he assured. 'Pa will be all right. I know he will.'

Mary Ann mustered a sad, fleeting smile. ''Course he will, son. He's a strong man, is your pa.'

They both looked at Isaac. Strong or

not, he appeared now to be a shell of himself. His face was pebbled with sweat and his lips continued to mouth words they neither could hear nor make sense of.

'I reckon I know what I got to do,' Will announced as if thinking aloud. 'I got to kill Charles Dunn.'

His mother stared at him. 'You can forget that foolishness,' she snapped. 'There's been violence enough as it is.'

'He picked a fight with Pa,' Will said. 'Him an' all them other Border Ruffians. And when Pa tried to get away Dunn stabbed him — in the back.' He shook his head as if still unable to believe it. 'I *am* gonna to kill him, Ma. An' what's more, the world will be a better place for it.'

'William Frederick Cody,' his mother said sternly, 'don't you *ever* let me hear you talk like that again.'

Will looked at her, his expression flat but unbowed. He didn't reply, but deep down he knew she was right. It *was* foolishness to think that he could get even with Charles Dunn. He was just a child, though he didn't feel like one right then, and doubted he would, ever again.

He went back to the corner and curled up in his blanket, knowing the only thing he could for now was sleep some more until his father had need of him again.

* * *

Isaac slept through the next day, and the one after that. And as every hour passed and his heart kept beating, Will dared to believe that he might pull through after all. Still, it was going to be a long while before his father returned to full strength, if ever. And so he set his uncharacteristic but still-consuming hatred for Charles Dunn aside and did what he could to keep his younger brother and sisters in line, and make sure the farm kept running.

It was a tall order for a boy not yet ten years old, but he did as much as he could and more besides, and all the while waited anxiously for the moment when his Pa would open his eyes again and tell them he was better; that he was going to be all right.

Half a week passed in that fashion, until late one afternoon Elijah rode in astride a stocky quarter horse. 'How is he?' he asked when Mary Ann let him into the parlor.

'Weak,' she replied. 'He sleeps most of the time. I've been trying to get him to take liquids, but it's hard. And food . . . well, there's no way he can eat, leastways not yet awhile.'

It was only then that she saw something in Elijah's his long, bearded face that she'd missed upon his arrival.

'What is it?' she asked. 'What's wrong?'

'They're coming for him,' Elijah said grimly. 'They're comin' to finish him.'

She swayed a little, whispered: 'What?'

Will stepped forward. 'Dunn?' he asked.

'The pro-slavers,' Elijah replied. 'They're callin' themselves the Kickapoo Rangers now — and it makes me sick to the stomach, the way they're behavin'.'

'I don't understand,' said Mary Ann. 'Haven't they done enough damage?'

'Your boy there's right,' said Elijah, turning his hat in his hands. 'Charlie Dunn's behind it. Way I hear tell, he's been showing up at the homes of the men who were there that day, saying as how they weren't just witnesses to what he did, that in the eyes of the law they'll be seen as accomplices. That's not true, of course — '

'They didn't have to watch it,' Will broke in. 'They could have stopped it.'

And when he looked at his uncle, his eyes said: You *could have stopped it.*

'I'll grant you that,' Elijah said, turning away. 'But Dunn's convinced the others — most of 'em, anyway — that they have to finish Isaac for good before he can lay charges of attempted murder against 'em.'

Mary Ann looked confused. The previous day a chamber pot and pin drummer had passed through and left them a copy of the *Democratic Reform*.

The newspaper had reported the attack, but not in any way that was likely to ensure that justice was done:

A Mr. Cody, a noisy abolitionist, living near Salt Creek, in Kansas Territory, was severely stabbed while in a dispute about a claim with a Mr. Dunn, on Monday week last. Cody is severely hurt, but not enough it is feared to cause his death. The settlers on Salt Creek regret that his wound is not more dangerous, and all sustain Mr. Dunn in the course he took.

'Do they really think anyone would make them answer to such a charge?' she asked scathingly.

'Could be,' Elijah replied. 'Kansas is gettin' ready to enter the Union, don't forget. The territory might not be welcome if it appears to condone attempted murder. Sooner or later Washington might demand that someone pay the price for what happened to Isaac.'

He didn't bother to mention the pure, mean cussedness Charles Dunn harbored for Isaac, regardless of politics.

'So they're coming,' whispered Mary Ann. 'These 'Kickapoo Rangers.''

'They're comin',' Elijah confirmed.

She looked at him, a woman at the end of her string. 'What are we going to do?'

'I'd take him to my place, if I thought he could survive the journey.'

'He won't. He's nowhere near up to that.'

'Then we'll have to hide him here, someplace.'

'Where?' asked Julia, coming closer. She was the image of her mother, though life hadn't yet had the chance to wear her down so thoroughly.

Elijah shook his head. 'The mood they're in, they'll tear this place apart, Mary. Your outbuildin's too.'

'Then we'll take him out into the cornfield,' said Will.

They all looked down at him. 'Don't be ridiculous, child,' said his mother.

Will disagreed. 'Ma,' he said firmly, 'the corn's about as high as it's likely to get. We flatten a patch right in the middle, no one'll guess where he is, an' we can take turns watchin' over him 'til he's strong enough to decide what to do for himself.'

'I think Will's right, Ma,' put in Julia. 'It's the last place anyone'd think to look for him.'

Elijah nodded. 'So do I. The nights are mild, so he won't have any problems with the cold. And you, Julia and young Will here can take turns out there, watchin' over him. He might be a touch uncomfortable for a while, but better that than . . . ' He left the remainder of the sentence unsaid, and covered it with: 'Come on — I don't know when they're like to come, so the sooner we get him settled out there the better.'

They hurried upstairs while the younger children watched them and wondered uneasily what was going on. Isaac was in bed, pale and sweaty. Elijah looked at him and wanted to weep with shame. When Isaac opened his blood-shot eyes, his brother saw the true extent of his suffering, and it was enormous.

Briefly, he told Isaac what they were going to do. It was hard to know just how much of it Isaac understood. Certainly he was too weak to raise any objection.

Next they wrapped a shawl around him and carefully walked him out of the cabin. Will pushed a way into the cornfield, making sure that the stalks would spring back into place behind them and betray no sign of their passing. Although he didn't know it at the time, the smell in there — reminiscent by turns of honey and dirt — would haunt him the rest of his life.

Once in the middle of the field he and Elijah stamped out an area big enough for Isaac to lie down on, and Mary Ann covered him with a blanket.

Now all they could do was wait for Charles Dunn and his fellow Border Ruffians to show up.

It didn't take long.

7

A little after midnight the family awoke to the sound of gunfire.

Will leaped off his bed and raced to the window. Outside, he saw a group of men riding back and forth outside the cabin, some holding burning torches, others shooting the Cody's pigs and chickens. Most of them were liquored-up, as they had been the day of the stabbing, and were laughing and whooping at the tops of their lungs.

The noise was deafening: the constant blast of handguns, the terrified squeal of pigs, the stamp and whinny of horses and —

Will stiffened.

Turk was running between riders, snapping and barking in an attempt to chase them off. One of the riders, a hulking, slightly stooped man who dwarfed the horse he was riding aimed a long-barreled revolver at the dog and fired once.

'*No!*' screamed Will.

But it was too late. The bullet hurled Turk two or three yards away. He howled, twitched a few times . . . then stopped moving altogether.

Will, sick inside, heard footsteps descending the stairs outside. His frightened sisters were crying for their mother. Will hurried from the room and went downstairs to join them.

His mother was standing in the center of the parlor floor, hugging young Charles to her breast and rocking him back and forth to stop him crying. 'Children!' she hissed. 'Go back upstairs and hide under your beds until I say otherwise!'

But it was too late for that. The front door smashed open and Charles Dunn burst inside, having to duck to avoid the head jamb.

Four-year-old May screamed, and that only made the baby cry harder.

Frozen with fear, Will looked up at the giant newcomer. Dunn seemed even taller and more frightening than Will remembered.

Dunn turned slowly to take in the room, the low lamplight throwing his shadow up across the wall and ceiling behind him. Outside, the shooting gradually tapered off, to be replaced by the odd stamp of hooves and the occasional sound of a restless horse blowing air through its nostrils.

At last Dunn fixed Mary Ann with glittering eyes and hissed: 'Where is he?'

Though terrified, she squared her shoulders and continued to rock her crying baby. 'Where you'll never find him.'

Dunn cocked his head. 'Dead?'

'No,' Mary Ann said. 'But a long way from here. And a long way from you.'

Not believing that, Dunn came deeper into the room and took another look around. The children stared up at him, wide-eyed and scared.

Will, standing at the foot of the stairs, thought about Julia and hoped she would stay put out in the field with Pa. If she came racing back to the house, she'd give away his father's hiding-place.

Then he realized that Dunn was looking down at him, and that he was staring right back, not averting his eyes, nor stepping aside. For a moment a hint of uncertainty crossed Dunn's jowly face at this show of defiance. Then Dunn pulled his knife from his jacket pocket — the same knife with which he'd stabbed Isaac.

'See this?' he rasped, holding the knife so close to Will he could see his own frightened eyes reflected in the blade. 'I been sharpenin' the edge so's I could finish the job I started las' week. Now — where's your pa, boy?'

Forcing the words around the lump in his throat, Will said: 'Think I'd tell you?'

Without warning, Dunn angrily back-handed him aside. Mary Ann cried out as Will fell hard against the wall. Ignoring her, Dunn quickly climbed the stairs. Each tread groaned beneath his weight.

One by one the Codys looked up at

the ceiling, listening as Dunn went from room to room, searching for his quarry and overturning furniture just for the hell of it. The only one who didn't follow Dunn's progress as he worked his way through the house was Will.

He crossed to the dresser, opened a drawer —

'*Boy!*' snapped Dunn, returning downstairs. 'What're you fussin' at over there?'

Will turned back to him, his father's big Walker Colt held tight in both hands.

'*This,*' he replied.

And to emphasize the word, he managed to thumb the big hammer back.

Mary Ann's eyes went wide. '*Will!*'

Dunn himself blanched. 'Set that smoke-wheel aside,' he barked.

That wasn't in Will's plans. 'You come and make me,' he dared.

'For chrissake, boy, I got a small army out there! You fire that gun — '

'I'm not worried about your army,' Will replied. 'Whatever they do to me after you're dead won't do a thing to fetch *you* back to life.'

Dunn's teeth clenched. 'You damn' whelp! You set that gun down!'

'I'll do just that,' said Will. 'After you and your friends get off our land. And if you ever come back, I'll use it.'

Part of him wanted to use it anyway. He'd said he planned to make Charles Dunn pay for what he'd done: he doubted that he'd ever get a better chance than this. And yet . . .

And yet he *couldn't* do it. Not this way, in front of his mother, his brother and his sisters. He couldn't do it right here, in cold blood, in their parlor. He couldn't do anything that would make their situation so much worse.

Still, Dunn didn't know that. Will could see that the big man was trying to decide whether or not he was bluffing. As booze-brave as he was right then, however, Dunn had no desire to find out. Putting his knife away, he stamped back out into the night, the door slamming shut behind him.

Will sagged with relief. He moved to

the window and saw Dunn mount his horse, whirl the animal around and ride off with his killing party.

Then Will lowered the hammer of the gun, put the weapon back in the drawer and went outside to bury Turk.

* * *

Although Will kept a careful watch after that, Dunn and his 'Kickapoo Rangers' didn't bother them again. But Will and his family knew it was only a matter of time before Dunn and his men came back.

Meanwhile, making ends meet became increasingly difficult. The family lived on what rabbits and birds that he was able to trap, supplemented by sod corn grated into flour. And powerless to do anything to improve their situation, Isaac could only continue to hide away in the cornfield, and allow his family to feed and care for him.

In low spirits, his health took a marked downward turn.

One afternoon, while Mary Ann watched over her husband, she put it to him that maybe he should think about hiding out in Grasshopper Falls until he finished healing.

Isaac lay quiet for a moment, considering. Mary Ann still found the change in him shocking, for though he was improving by the day, he was still thin, weak and restricted in his mobility by the slow-healing wound. The idea of moving anywhere was probably more than he could manage right then, but Grasshopper Falls was almost home from home. Isaac had been one of the founders of the still-new town, and there was serious talk that, like the town of Lawrence, it would eventually become a haven for Free Staters. As such, Isaac would probably be safer there than anywhere.

'Let me think on it a spell,' he said finally, his voice a husky croak. 'I'm not sure I got the journey in me, Mary.'

His wife couldn't fault him for that. Although she was only proposing a journey of twenty-five or thirty miles, it would seem far longer than that to a man in Isaac's condition.

'Well, we've got to do something,' she said. 'Will . . . '

'What about him?' Isaac asked as she stopped.

'That boy idolizes you,' she said gently. 'He took it awful hard when you got stabbed. And . . . ' She fell quiet again.

'What is it?' Isaac prodded. 'Dammit, woman, tell me!'

'He said he was goin' to kill Charles Dunn,' she blurted. 'He almost did it, too, a few nights ago.' Her eyes met his. 'I think he might still do it yet.'

She could see he was skeptical.

'He's only nine,' Isaac reminded.

'He was nine before Dunn tried to kill you,' she replied. 'After that he grew up.' She squeezed his arm: it was all bone beneath her palm. 'You've got to do what's right, Isaac. And what's right, right now, is to get back on your feet before that boy does something rash

. . . something he'll regret for the rest of his life.'

Isaac stared up at the sky. The smell of dirt and honey was strong around them as a balmy September wind chased itself through the cornstalks.

'You're right,' he said. 'Ah, hell, I've had my fill of layin' out here, starin' up at the sky, anyway. An' I've sure as wedlock had enough of bein' sick. I got to get well for you an' the family, like you say. But 'specially for Will, by the sounds of it. That boy needs his father. Without him, he's apt to run wild.'

He looked at her, and when she looked back, she tried not to see the way he had to labor for each breath, how even the slightest effort taxed him to the limit.

'Grasshopper Falls it is, Mary.'

'All right,' she said, relieved. 'You rest up now. I'll have words with Jim Lane. He'll help out and take you there, I know he will.'

Isaac had no doubt of that. Lane was not only a good neighbor; he was also a

Free Stater. He was bitterly opposed to the likes of Charles Dunn and his Kickapoo Rangers, and that made him a valuable ally indeed.

'Do it soon as you can,' he said. 'If what you say's true, an' Will does anything foolish now, we've lost him for good.'

8

How they did it and kept it a secret, Mary Ann would never know. But even in smuggling Isaac to Grasshopper Falls, Will played his part. On the night Jim Lane planned to sneak Isaac out of Leavenworth County, the boy took it upon himself to scout the land for several miles around before returning to home to give their neighbor the all clear. He also insisted on riding ahead of Lane's creaking Murphy wagon, still keeping a watchful eye on their surroundings with his father's Walker Colt stuffed into his waistband, until they were well across the county line.

In the early morning hours he returned home exhausted, but with the news that his father was now safely on his way to friends in Grasshopper Falls. The news lifted a great weight from his mother's weary shoulders.

It was two weeks before Lane, a short, wiry man with a chinstrap beard, paid them another visit. He confirmed Isaac's safe arrival in Grasshopper Falls and then produced an unopened letter that had been mailed to him in care of Riveley's Trading Post. He'd been expecting the letter, because Isaac had promised to put pen to paper at the earliest opportunity, and having recognized Isaac's handwriting, he'd brought it directly to Mary Ann.

The news was better than she could have hoped for. Isaac was eating well and putting on a little weight. Sleep was a whole heap easier on a feather mattress than it had been on hard ground, and he suspected that this, too, was playing its part in his recovery. He said that Grasshopper Falls was expanding well, and the saw-mill he had helped to build was in great demand. As he had predicted at the time, the Grasshopper River had turned out to be a fine source of power for the mill.

Mary Ann wept tears of joyful relief.

Though she would never say as much, things were nowhere near as rosy for her and the family. The Codys were still finding it hard to make ends meet, and on several occasions a man named Sharpe, a heavy drinker who acted as the local justice of the peace and was a known supporter of Charles Dunn and his Kickapoo Rangers, had called in unannounced to demand a meal. Not wanting trouble, Mary Ann had always supplied one from their meager larder.

At the end of every visit, Sharpe always asked after Isaac. All Mary Ann would ever say was that: 'He is no longer with us.'

It was up to Sharpe how he interpreted that.

'Well, at this rate I 'spect Isaac will be back home soon,' Lane remarked, breaking in on her thoughts. 'I know that'll please young Will. How is the boy, anyhow?'

'Poorly,' Mary Ami replied. 'He's run himself ragged ever since Dunn stabbed his father. Could barely crawl out of his bed this mornin'.'

'Too bad,' said Lane. 'He's a boy to be proud of.'

'He is, that,' she admitted. 'But if I know Will, it'll take more than the grippe to keep down for long.'

Even so, Will was confined to bed for the next several days. A dry cough kept him awake at night, and during the day he alternated between fever and chills. When he did manage to sleep, his dreams were haunted by images of Charles Dunn and his knife. Dunn's attack on his father replayed itself endlessly through his delirious mind, and all he could do was watch helplessly as his father froze in mid-pace, agony crushing his features, and say over and over again: *Pa! Oh Lordy, Pa, what've they done to you?*

As his health improved the nightmares faded, and when he woke up one morning at the end of that week, he knew at once that he was going to be all right. His head felt clearer, and the persistent ache in his limbs had all but vanished. For once, sitting up didn't make him want to puke. He was just tired now, that was all.

As he washed his face, he heard voices coming from downstairs — those of a man and a woman. Still drowsy, he somehow convinced himself that his father was downstairs: that his father had come home and that from now on everything was going to be all right. Galvanized by the notion, he left his room and stumbled down to the parlor.

His father was nowhere to be seen. But Uncle Elijah was sitting on the sofa, talking to Mary Ann. They both looked around when a tread creaked beneath him, and Mary Ann stood up. He saw at once that she had been crying.

'Will!' she said, quickly wiping at her eyes. 'You shouldn't be up, you're — '

Will cut her off. 'I'm all right, Ma. I'm better.' He looked at his uncle. 'Is my pa all right, Uncle Lije? Is that why you're here?'

Elijah looked at Mary Ann and then he stood up. 'I reckon you better go back to bed, son.'

'What's wrong? Is my pa — ?'

Mary Ann said: 'Your father sent us a letter earlier this week. He figured it was safe enough to send it to Mr. Lane, care of Riveley's.'

Will blinked, still trying to force his sluggish brain to work. 'Wasn't it?'

'It couldn't've been,' said Elijah. 'Someone somewhere must've recognized his fist an' checked the return address.' His mouth tightened. 'Now Dunn knows where to find him — an' the word is he's gatherin' his Rangers to finish the job once an' for all.'

Will gasped. 'Then he's got to be warned!'

Elijah nodded. 'I'm on my way to Grasshopper Falls right now. I just stopped by to let your ma know what's — '

Will glanced out the window into the yard. 'It'll take you forever in a wagon.'

'Don't fret, son, I'll warn him in good time — '

Ignoring him, Will turned and, grabbing the banister rail, started pulling himself back up to his room.

His mother took a step toward the staircase. 'Will?'

'Me an' Prince will make the journey in half the time,' Will called back to her.

'Will Cody, you're not going anywhere except straight back to bed!'

The boy didn't reply.

Ten minutes later he came back downstairs fully dressed. His mother was still there waiting for him.

'Young man — ' she began.

But when he looked up at her she fell silent, because while he had certainly become a man over the past few weeks, there seemed to be nothing left in him now that could be described as *young*.

'Will . . . ' Elijah said warningly. 'Best you pay heed to your mother.'

Stubbornly, Will went past him to the dresser, opened the drawer and took out his father's Walker Colt.

'You're not going anywhere, Will!' said Mary Ann. 'Especially not with that weapon!'

'Oh, yes I am,' he replied stubbornly.

'And no one's going t' stop me!'

And within a few minutes, he galloped off on his favorite horse.

★ ★ ★

The horizon in that part of the territory was an even split between grass and sky. To anyone unused to it, the sheer vastness of the open country could inspire awe and fear in near-equal measure. Arrowfeather grass waved stiffly in the constant breeze, broken here and there by equally immense swathes of slender bluestem and Jimsonweed, milkweed and yarrow. Trees were rare, and when they did spring up they were usually post oak or blackjack. Principally, however, this was a land of brush: of Russian olive and wild plum, elderberry and salt cedar.

Right then Will had eyes for only the trail ahead. All that mattered was that he reached Grasshopper Falls in time to warn his father of the danger he was in.

But that wasn't going to be an easy

task. As the miles unwound beneath them and Prince's black coat began to fleck with foam, Will started to feel faint. He was sweaty and empty-bellied, and he knew that yet again his mother had been right — he'd been in no condition to make this ride.

But what choice did he have? There was none that he could see. And so he rode on, pushing himself and his horse until at last he had no option but to rein up, slide from the saddle and hunker down and vomit.

Prince waited beside Will until the nausea passed and the boy felt a little better again. Then he pulled himself up, found the stirrup, remounted and rode on.

After a time he spotted a stand of trees to the northeast and knew he was close to a shallow, nameless tributary of the Delaware. Water seemed like a real good idea right then, and he guided Prince toward it.

It was now well into October, but the Kansas heat was still hard on man and beast. The timber, when he reached it, provided welcome shade. And when he saw sunlight rippling off the stream just beyond the spot where the trees thinned out, he licked his parched lips in anticipation.

At last boy and horse reached the grassy bank. Will, exhausted and feeling faint, started to dismount and almost fell from the saddle. His joints ached fiercely. He took off his hat, flopped onto his belly and started to scoop water over his face. Beside him, Prince drank thirstily.

'*Look!*' a voice yelled

Startled, Will got up, all weariness suddenly forgotten. Looking to his right, he spotted a group of men watering their horses about a quarter-mile further downstream. He recognized them at once as Dunn's Kickapoo Rangers.

'*It's Cody's kid!*' yelled the same man.

Will scrambled up and leapt back into the saddle just as one of the Rangers fired a shot at him. It missed. And before anyone could fire again, Prince leaped into the stream. Will clung on, white water exploding all around him, the horse plunging toward the safety of the far timbered bank.

Another gunshot sounded. Will grabbed for the Colt in his waistband, intending to return fire. As he dragged the weapon free, however, it slipped from his wet hand and vanished into the water.

'Damn!'

He couldn't leave the weapon there — it belonged to his pa!

Quickly he dismounted, bent and snatched the gun up off the pebble-strewn stream bottom. Shoving it back into his waistband, he turned back to the horse and toed into the stirrup. Prince, unnerved by the shouts and gunfire, turned in a skittish circle, delaying him for precious seconds.

'Hold still, you knothead!'

'You — Cody!'

Finally swinging back astride, Will saw Charles Dunn racing along the bank, sunshine glinting off the Bowie knife in his right hand.

'Rein up, you little bastard!' Dunn yelled, and when he was near enough he threw himself into the stream and started wading through the knee-high water to reach his quarry.

Terrified now, Will went to spur Prince on. But before he could, he took another look at Dunn and this time he flared hot with rage.

Dunn.

This man had tried to kill his father.

He'd shot Turk dead.

Dunn had intimidated his entire family and been responsible for forcing his father to leave his home.

Dunn had haunted Will's dreams for a week now, turning them into nightmares.

And that was when Will thought: *No more.*

Impulsively he turned Prince and started galloping along the center of the stream to meet the man who even now was raising the knife high over his head. He felt his mouth wrench wide and his cry — 'Yahhh! Yahhh!' — echoed between the trees.

The distance closed rapidly. Man and horse somehow missed colliding in that first charge. Then Will felt pain sear through his right leg, just above the knee, and looking down saw that he'd been cut. He realized Dunn had sliced him as they passed.

The knowledge only increased the anger that was wholly at odds with his tender years. He dragged at the reins and Prince reared up and turned, and the second he came down again Will had him charging back toward Dunn.

Dunn, his long-held hatred of the Codys now blinding him to all else, had also stopped and turned. Planting himself in the middle of the stream, he hurled the knife at Will. It flew end over end and Will pressed himself flat against the horse's pumping neck to avoid it. The blade went past and splashed into the water behind him.

But Will kept Prince going, going, going —

The horse slammed into Dunn,

sending him flying backward. His scream choked off as his mouth filled with water.

Will turned Prince again, clenching his teeth against the pain in his leg. Once more Will spurred the horse onward. And Prince churned through the water, spray, backlit by the sun, exploding all around him.

Dunn had resurfaced, his massive shoulders rising and falling, water dripping from him. He cursed Will and drew a Colt that must be the next thing to useless after its dunking.

Even as he brought the weapon up and thumbed back the hammer, Prince hit him again, and this time the force was such that it made the horse stagger. Dunn himself pulled the trigger. The Colt actually fired, sending a bullet slapping down into the water beside him.

Then Dunn pitched over backward.

While Prince recovered, Will leaned sideways and once again dry-heaved.

It was while he was leaning over that

Dunn slowly floated past him, on his back, his eyes open and unblinking, his broad chest now caved in. Blood ran from the big man's ears, nose and mouth. It swirled around him like red smoke.

He was dead.

Will pushed himself upright again, and fighting the urge to pass out, looked downstream at the rest of the Rangers.

Awed by what they'd just seen, they stood in stunned silence. If they wanted him now, he was theirs for the taking. He'd used up all his energy and his cut leg was throbbing painfully.

But the Kickapoo Rangers made no move toward Will.

Surprised, he wondered how this thing would go now. He could only hope that with Dunn, the driving force, no longer behind them, the determination of these men to see his father dead would, itself, die.

He watched as the Rangers caught up Dunn's body and dragged it ashore.

They wrapped Dunn in a blanket and several of them lifted him up and tied him across his horse.

Will urged Prince closer, and called out: 'I never meant for this to happen!'

The Rangers only looked at him.

'Me and my folks would've sooner done without all this trouble!' Will added. Inside, the boy in him wanted to cry, but the man held the tears in check. 'Sensible folks would say it ends right here, I reckon!'

The Rangers silently watched him for a while longer. A few of them exchanged glances, then words, and then there were nods of agreement all round. One of the Rangers lifted a hand, almost in grudging salute, and then let it drop. After that the Rangers mounted up and rode back toward Leavenworth County.

Will sagged.

It was over.

God help him — it was over.

Part Three — Cowboy

9

But the killing of Charles Dunn could hardly be called a victory. The death of no man could ever be called that. And neither, in the end, was it of any benefit to Isaac Cody.

When Isaac returned home in the spring of 1857, it became obvious that all his talk of recovery had been just that — talk. In truth, he was a shade of his former self. Weakened not only by the knife wound but also by a recent bout of scarlet fever, he died within a matter of months. He was forty-six years old.

Under any other circumstances, that would have left Will as the man of the house. But Will had already been the man of the house for several months now. His father's death only confirmed what he himself already knew: that he must find paying work if his family were to survive.

One day, while talking to the captain of a passing bull-train, he learned that Congress had dispatched an army expedition to Utah, under the command of General William S. Harney and Colonel Albert Sidney Johnston. There'd been trouble with the Mormons, the captain said, and having been driven out of their previous strongholds in Ohio, Illinois and Missouri, the Church of Jesus Christ of Latter-day Saints was determined to keep Utah — what they themselves called 'Deseret' — at any cost. This included violence, cattle rustling and the cold-blooded slaughter of Gentiles or any other outsiders on a shocking scale. A private Mormon army known as the Danites, or 'Destroying Angels', were said to have committed the outrages.

The news was of no special consequence to Will until he learned that Russell, Majors & Waddell had been awarded a contract to keep the U. S. Army expedition supplied. Then he was quick to spot a chance for employment.

Early the following day he saddled

Prince and rode to the freight company offices in Leavenworth. Here, not knowing any better, he requested an interview with Alexander Majors himself.

Curious to see what the boy wanted, Majors — in his mid-forties, handsome in a bullish kind of way and impeccably dressed in a tailored business suit as black as his thick, curly hair — agreed to hear him out.

But when Will finished, Majors only eyed him with amusement. 'There's just one problem, Master Cody,' he said without malice. 'You're only a boy. And we don't hire boys.'

Will had been expecting that. 'I can't deny my age, Mr. Majors. But I need that job. My folks are in a bad way. We lost my pa and — '

That stirred a memory in Majors. 'Cody?' he interrupted. 'He was the Free Stater, wasn't he?'

'Yes, sir.'

'Thought so. I heard about what happened, and it was a damn' shame.

I'm sorry for your loss, boy. And I'd give you work if I could. But tell me . . . what can you do?'

'I know how to handle horses real well.'

'I've already got wranglers.'

'Well . . . what about cattle? They say you're runnin' beef west along with your supplies. Couldn't I help drive the herd?'

Majors studied him for a moment, clearly seeing the desperation Will was trying so hard to hide. 'I've got men to drive the cattle, son . . . but I suppose I can always use one more.'

'Thank you, sir! You won't regret it!'

'Forty dollars a month,' Majors continued, 'which I will pay directly to your mother.'

It was the best news Will had heard in a long time. 'I won't let you down, Mr. Majors! My word on it!'

'You know something, Master Cody? I believe you.'

'Do I have time to go back home and say goodbye to my folks, sir?'

'If you don't tarry,' Majors replied. 'The train pulls out day after tomorrow. That's Wednesday. Be back here by seven o'clock on Wednesday morning . . . or it will leave without you.'

★　★　★

True to his word, Will was outside the freight company warehouse when Alexander Majors arrived to open up at seven o'clock on Wednesday morning. Upon entering his office, Majors took a book from the shelf behind his desk and handed it to the boy.

'Can you read, Master Cody?'

'Tolerably, sir. And do my ciphers.'

'Good lad. There's a card tucked just inside the book. Take it out, and with the book held tight in your right hand, read what's on it.'

Will frowned. 'Excuse me?'

'There's a space at the beginning,' Majors continued, as if he hadn't heard the question. 'You say your full name where that space appears.'

Will looked at the book and realized for the first time that it was a Bible. He took the dog-eared card from inside the cover and looked at it a moment. Then, awkwardly, he read:

'I, William Frederick Cody, do hereby swear, before the Great and Living God, that during my en . . . engagement, and while I am an employee of Russell, Majors, and Waddell, I will, under no circum . . . stances, use profane language; that I will drink no in . . . in-tox-i-cating liquors: that I will not quarrel or fight with any other employee of the firm, and that in every respect I will conduct myself honestly, be faithful to my duties, and so direct all my acts as to win the . . . confidence . . . of my employers, so help me God.'

Majors took the Bible from him and offered his hand. 'Now it's official, Master Cody. Welcome to the company.'

Majors then took him through the warehouse and introduced him to the wagon-master, a big, solemn man of fifty whom he introduced as Lew Simpson.

Simpson was every inch a plainsman. His seamed face was burned to the color of an old penny by prairie winds, his thick, wavy beard showing prematurely gray where it wasn't stained brown by chewing tobacco. Clad in loose-fitting, fringed buckskins and well-worn moccasins, he covered his shoulder-length graying hair with a high-crowned, flat-brimmed felt hat. Wedged behind his quilled belt, cross-draw fashion, were two Colt Model 1855 revolvers.

'You know Mr. Majors well?' Simpson asked Will after Majors had returned to the office.

'No, sir.'

'Well, he seems to know you — or leastways know *of* you. Says you're a regular snake-stomper.'

'I'm not, sir. Honest.'

'He also tells me you killed a man a few months back.'

'Five months back, an' it was me or him,' Will replied bleakly. 'I didn't take any pleasure from it, but as much as any man needs killin', he did, I reckon.'

Simpson studied him for a long beat, getting his measure. 'I'll have to take your word for that, since I don't know the circumstances,' he said at length. 'But be told, boy, there's no place for troublemakers on this trip. We got the better part of a thousand miles to go, right across the good Territory of Colorado and beyond. Be a heap easier if everyone gets along.'

'I don't want trouble, sir. My word on it.'

Satisfied by that, Simpson stuck out one large hand and they shook. He was impressed by the firmness of the boy's grip. 'Catch up your horse, son. We aim to leave at noon, so let's get you settled in before we pull out.'

* * *

As Leavenworth fell behind them, Will thought about the life he had known to this point and the uncertainty of what lay ahead. As he'd expected, saying

114

goodbye to his mother had been hell. Indeed, just the memory of it still brought a lump to his throat.

As if the family hadn't suffered enough already, his mother — herself worn down by the events of the previous several months — had contracted consumption. Due to the infectious nature of the illness, the local doctor had advised her to keep her distance from her children. He'd also suggested that she eat as well as her funds allowed, but to stop eating meat, and seriously consider moving to a milder climate. If all that failed, they might consider surgery, deliberately collapsing her lungs in the hope that the resulting 'rest' would bring about a cure.

All of which meant that Will was forced to say his goodbyes from her bedroom doorway. She wouldn't allow him to come any closer. And even though her curtains were closed and the room was mostly in shadow, there could be no mistaking how frail she looked beneath the coverlet; how thin, fragile and bloodless.

'Mr. Majors says he'll make sure you get my wages,' he said, to break the heavy silence that had followed his announcement.

'I wish it didn't . . . have to be like this,' she replied. Her voice was tired and hoarse, and though her cough had subsided for the time being, he knew the next fit would leave her gasping for breath and choking blood into a cloth, as it always did.

'Well, I reckon we all wish that, Ma. But it is what it is, as Pa used to say. Just have to make the best of it.'

She smiled fondly at him. 'Will Cody,' she said gently. 'You always were the apple of your Pa's eye. If he could see you now, how you've grown up . . . how you've *had* to grow up . . . why, he'd be as proud as a prince.'

Will, hearing that, experienced a sudden, overpowering surge of emotion and he desperately wanted to go and hug her. But he knew she wouldn't

116

allow it, not in her present state. So all he said, thickly, was: 'I guess I better get my gear together, then. Got to be in Leavenworth bright an' early, or they'll go without me, they say.'

She nodded, her face ghostly white except for the two bright fever spots high on her cheeks. 'Look after yourself, Will,' she said. 'Write as often as you can. An' come back to us in one piece.'

'I'll do that,' he promised.

'Will?' she added as he turned to leave.

'Yes, Ma?'

'I love you, son.'

'I love you, Ma.'

And because neither of them wanted to acknowledge the tears in the other's eyes, he turned and hurried out.

10

'You all right, there, Will?' asked Simpson.

Clearing his throat, Will sat straighter in his saddle. 'Yes, sir.'

'You seem awful quiet all of a sudden,' the burly captain noted. 'Havin' second thoughts?'

'No, sir,' he lied.

'How old are you, Will?'

'Ten, sir.'

'That's a tender age, even out here,' said Simpson. He hesitated, then said with some embarrassment: 'You have any trouble on this trail, you come see me, y'hear?'

'Yes, sir.'

'I mean it, son. You might've just left one family, but you've now been taken into another. Any time you feel you can't handle it, you come find me. We'll chaw on it a spell and see what's to be done with you.'

'Yes, sir. Thank you.'

'An' quit calling me 'sir', will you? I'm Mr. Simpson to you.'

'Yes, si . . . Mr. Simpson.'

'Now,' said Simpson, 'eyes forward, son. There she is.'

As they crested a rise, Will saw the wagon train assembled in the valley below them and caught his breath.

Twenty-five Conestoga wagons, each painted sky-blue and weighing about a ton, were lined up in two parallel columns across the horse-belly-high grass, white canvas bonnets rippling in the keen April wind. Each wagon had six massive oxen in its traces. Men in shirtsleeves were busily checking wheels, axles and brake blocks, while half a dozen of Simpson's lieutenants galloped back and forth, making sure that preparations for their leaving continued apace.

Almost a quarter-mile beyond the last of the wagons Will spotted an enormous herd of longhorn cattle. They formed a shifting sea of color that ranged from speckled blue-gray to brown, black and, predominantly, dark red and white.

Without realizing it, he whistled softly.

'Ever seen a longhorn before, Will?'

'No, sir. I reckon I'd remember seein' a critter like that.'

Simpson laughed. 'Yessir, I reckon you would.'

Rangy and long-legged, the steers stood five or so feet to the hipbone and Will estimated they must weigh between eight hundred pounds to more than a thousand. But it was their horns that captivated him most of all. Some of the cattle down there — particularly the older ones — boasted horn-spans of six or seven feet from tip to tip. Even from this distance, he could hear the way they clicked and clacked against each other as the cattle shifted around.

'That's about eight hundred head you're lookin' at,' said Simpson. 'One day I daresay we'll move 'em by the thousands, but for now that's a pretty fair size.'

They rode down into the valley, along

the line of wagons and then skirted the blatting herd until they reached a stalled chuck wagon, beside which a small group of cowboys were drinking coffee. When they saw the boy with Simpson, their curiosity showed plain.

'Mr. Parsons,' said Simpson as they drew rein and swung down, 'this here's Will Cody, from up Salt Creek way. He's gonna help you push your herd to Utah.'

Parsons was a short, lean-flanked man with a dark complexion and bowed legs. He was about thirty, with a constant stubble and skin like dried leather. 'Oh, you *are*, are you?' he asked good-naturedly.

'Yes, sir.'

The trail-boss and his men were all dressed in pretty much the same fashion — placket shirts, either striped or of a single color, and canvas pants or Levi's tucked into high-heeled stovepipe boots. Every man wore a broad-brimmed hat and went armed. Indicating each one in turn, Parsons said: 'That there's Pete Johnson . . . Sam Heywood . . . Ethan

Starch ... Ira Thomas ... an' Lyle Reese. Feller over yonder, by the wagon, that's Cheater Webb. You keep on Cheater's sweet side an' you'll never go hungry. You'll meet the rest of the crew later.'

The cook and four of the drovers exchanged perfunctory nods of greeting. But the last man, Reese, only spat.

Noticing that, Simpson asked: 'You got a problem there, Reese?'

Reese was in his mid-twenties, with a long, narrow face and a sour mouth beneath an untrimmed mustache the color of sand. His hair was fair and shaggy, his eyes a cold blue, and there was a kink in his nose, about halfway down, where it had once been broken and never properly reset.

'A kid around usually means double work for the rest of us,' he replied.

'Not this kid,' Simpson assured him. 'He'll carry his weight.'

'Will he, now?'

'My word on it,' said Simpson. He cocked his head to one side. 'Anythin' else?'

122

Reese only spat again, the gesture one of clear defiance. Before the situation could escalate, however, Parsons said: 'That's good enough for us, Mr. Simpson. All right, fellers, I'm pretty sure you all got work to do! As for *you*, sprout,' he said to Will, 'stow your gear in back of the chuck wagon an' we'll make a start on your education.'

When Will had done as told, and the rest of the men had mounted and ridden out, Parsons explained that the object of the drive was to drift the cattle along at a pace that covered plenty of ground but also allowed them to retain their weight.

'No point in us deliverin' a bunch of skeletons to them soldier boys,' he said. 'They'll be wantin' meat, not bone.' Indicating the herd with a sweep of one rope-scarred hand, he went on: 'After today, we'll rest 'em every noon and again overnight. But there won't be much rest for *you*, sprout. You'll do your share of nighthawkin' too, before we get where we're goin'. For now, though, you'll be ridin' drag.'

'Yes, sir,' said Will. And then: 'Uh . . . what's 'ridin' drag', Mr. Parsons?'

The trail boss sighed. 'I ride up front. Rest of the men I send out there, there, and there. That's point, swing and flank, you got it? *Drag* is when a man brings up the rear, keeps the cattle ahead of him movin' an' watches out for bunch-quitters. I won't dress it up, sprout. It's the worst job I can give you, but there's no malice in it. We all got to start somewhere.'

'I understand, Mr. Parsons.'

'Glad to hear it. You got a spare bandanna?'

'Yes, sir.'

'Well, you make sure you tie it around your mouth an' nose, against the dust, 'cause, trust me, you'll be covered in it by day's end.'

'Can't I use the one I'm wearing now, sir?'

'No sir, you cannot. You leave that one right where it is or else the sun will just about fry your neck.' He grinned. 'Now, hop to it, sprout. Oh, an' one other thing.'

'Yes, sir?'

Parsons' expression sobered, and even though there was no need, he lowered his voice. 'Don't mind Reese overmuch. He's heard your name before, just like I have; I saw it plain on his face when Mr. Simpson introduced you. Only difference is, I'm Free State, like your pa was. Reese *ain't*. Him an' his folks're Border Ruffian to the core, an' I reckon you know better'n most just how hard a Border Ruffian can hate.'

Will swallowed. 'I don't want no trouble, Mr. Parsons. I took an oath not to quarrel or fight.'

'We all take that oath, sprout — Alexander Majors insists on it. But you remember one thing. There's a world o' difference between pickin' a fight and stickin' up for yourself. So don't take no guff from Reese or he'll make your life hell.'

Will was still thinking about that

when, close to noon, Simpson sent his lieutenants back along the line to say that they were finally moving out. A string of cries echoed the length of the train's two columns, and these, coupled with the sudden, restless stirring of the herd, sent a jolt of excitement through him. One after another, the Conestoga drivers got their oxen moving, and big, red-painted wagon wheels slowly began to turn.

The trek was underway.

Parsons, meanwhile, circled the herd, checking that everyone was where they should be. Cheater Webb, driving the chuck wagon, was stationed at the head and a little to the left of the herd. Several hundred yards behind it came the remuda, with the wrangler, a cheerful nineteen-year-old named Ned Neeley, keeping a careful eye on the horses in his charge.

Expectancy filled the air, but Parsons didn't move them out immediately. He waited for the wagons to get a reasonable head start and then gave the order for the men to start pushing the herd at an easy walk behind them.

Bringing up the rear, Will glanced off to the northeast and home. With a sudden rush of sentiment, he wondered how his mother was doing right then; what his brother and sisters were up to. Above the line of his second bandanna, he felt his eyes mist, and for a moment considered turning Prince and just riding away; of going back home and trying to find some other way to earn money that didn't mean having to leave his mother when she was so ill.

Then he remembered that he'd sworn service to Alexander Majors, and that Simpson had assured Reese that he'd pull his weight. There was no way he would let either man down . . . and certainly no way he'd let *himself* down.

So, when the other two drag riders heeled their horses into the dust left behind by the herd, he was right there beside them, yelling, whistling and waving his hat back and forth like he'd been driving cattle all his life.

11

As used to the open spaces as he was, nothing could have prepared Will for the sheer enormity of the Great Plains. As the days passed and the wagon train crawled on across grasslands without end, he began to see that the land was nowhere near as flat as he had always believed. In truth, low hills topped with scrub, mesquite and sagebrush in almost every direction.

Beneath a cloudless blue sky that was so vast it was intimidating, wildlife also prospered. When he wasn't choking on dust or struggling to learn the cowboy craft, he spotted herds of pronghorn antelope and flocks of sharp-tailed grouse. Streams silvered the land in abundance, and sprawling prairie dog towns were just as plentiful. His lullaby at night was usually the yipping of coyotes.

There were pests too, of course; mostly rattlesnakes and chiggers — tiny mites that constantly bit him. But he bore every hardship without complaint. Complaining was not in his nature. And though he worked as hard as he could to justify the faith Majors and Simpson had shown in him, it seemed there was nothing he could do to win over Lyle Reese. The broken-nosed cowboy never missed a chance to belittle him, and whenever Will did something wrong, Reese was always the first to criticize him. Even the fact that Will was a fast learner seemed to infuriate Reese.

Within days, Will's already competent horsemanship had improved beyond recognition. He was soon capable of keeping the cattle moving and chasing bunch-quitters back toward the herd.

The fact that he was doing a man's job and doing it well wasn't lost on Parsons. The other men found themselves accepting him, too. But not Reese!

Never Reese!

Long before dusk fell on their fifth

day out Lew Simpson rode ahead, as he always did, to find a campsite. Having found it, he then made some quick mental calculations before marking out two wide, rough circles in the grass, one a short distance from the other. Will had no idea how he did it, but by the time the wagon-master finished guiding the last of the Conestogas into position, he always managed to form two near perfect, secure rings for the night.

Parsons, meanwhile, let the herd drink at one of the streams that always seemed to be nearby and then saw to bedding the steers down. With the sun setting fast now, and campfires taking hold, Will turned his horse in at the remuda and gave a jaw-cracking yawn. He was dead on his feet and would have been happy to curl up in his blankets if Parsons hadn't told him to eat first.

'Ache like hell, do you, sprout?' the trail-boss asked him.

'From my tip to my tailbone, sir.'

'Well, come and see me before you

turn in,' said Parsons. 'I'll give you a bottle of whiskey laced with salt water.'

Will hesitated. 'Uh . . . I can't drink no in-tox-i-catin' liquors, Mr. Parsons,' he said apologetically. 'I took an oath.'

The trail-boss laughed. 'You don't *drink* it, sprout, you rub it into your backside! It's the best damn' hide-toughener you can get!'

Blushing at his mistake, Will shuffled over to the chuck wagon.

'You did well today, Will,' called Pete Johnson.

'Real well,' confirmed Ira Thomas with a toothy grin. 'Why, I bet you jus' can't wait to do the whole thing all over again t'morry.'

Will took the plate of beans he was handed and wearily ate without bothering to taste the food. When he was finished, he dropped his plate into the wreck pan and was about to help himself to a dipper of water from the barrel attached to the side of the wagon when Reese, who'd been resting against his upturned saddle on the far side of the fire, called: 'Boy! Fetch me that coffee pot!'

The relaxed atmosphere changed instantly.

With the dipper partway to his mouth, Will looked around, determined to keep the fear he felt for his tormentor hidden.

Glaring back at him, Reese snapped: 'You slow between the ears, kid? I said, fetch me that pot!'

Around the fire, the other men waited uncomfortably to see what Will would do.

He didn't keep them waiting long.

'Fetch it yourself,' he said softly.

Reese's expression tightened. 'What was that?'

Hoping to break the mood, Sam Heywood forced a chuckle and said: 'That's tellin' you, Lyle — '

'Shut up!' Reese barked, not taking his eyes off Will. 'Seems to me you oughta show some respect for your betters, boy.'

He got up and stamped toward the

wagon. Will watched him come.

'When I tell you to do somethin',' growled Reese, 'best you hop to it, kid, else there'll be hell to pay.'

'Lyle . . . ' Thomas said warningly.

'You want more coffee, you get it yourself,' said Will, having to force the words out. 'I'm not your slave.'

And there it was — the word *slave*.

At last it was out in the open, the reason behind the instant dislike Reese had taken to him, and without warning Reese backhanded him. Startled, Will cried out, and the sound was like music to Reese's ears.

Ethan Starch quickly scrambled up. 'Judas Priest, Lyle, he's just a kid!'

But Reese ignored him. 'Now,' he said, digging his fingers deep into Will's jaw and glaring down into his face, 'next time I tell you to do somethin', you *do* it!'

Cheek already swelling, Will glared right back at him. 'You want a drink,' he said, 'have what's left in this.'

And he struck Reese around the face

with the dipper.

The blow sounded like billiard balls colliding. Reese staggered sideways, grabbing at an ear and cheekbone he could no longer feel. Then, with a bellow of rage, he threw himself back at Will, slapping him across the face with enough force to drop him to his knees.

'*Lyle* — !' yelled Thomas.

Ignoring him, Reese kicked the boy even as Will tried to curl into a protective ball, then brought his leg up with the intention of stomping him.

That was when someone grabbed his shoulder and spun him around.

He came face to face with a tall, spare man with long, sharp features and a clipped handlebar mustache.

Before Reese could say anything, the newcomer punched him in the face.

Reese collapsed, bleeding from the nose.

Content that Reese no longer posed any immediate threat, the sharp-featured man turned to Will. In his early twenties, he had long, curly ash-brown hair spilling from beneath a knitted liberty cap and wore the buckskins of a scout. A moment later he offered a hand and helped Will up.

'Little young to be pickin' fights, ain't you?' he remarked.

'I didn't pick it,' began Will, holding his side where Reese had kicked him. 'He — '

'I know,' interrupted the newcomer. 'I just rode in an' caught the tail-end of it.' He went on to explain that he'd been hired to help guide the train to Utah. But as he was talking, Will noticed that the man also carried twin Navy Colts with ivory grips and fancy silver plating tucked into his red sash. The distinctive guns, as well as the man's cold, flat stare, suggested another, more sinister occupation.

'I'll say this,' the man continued, 'you got sand, I'll give you that. You got a name to go with it, youngster?'

'Cody,' said Will. 'Will Cody.'

'Pleased to meet you, Will Cody. My name's Hickok. James Butler Hickok.

But my friends call me Wild Bill.'

Without waiting for an acknowledgement, Hickok hunkered down and gave Reese a rough shake. Slowly, reluctantly, Reese came round. Not sure where he was, he clawed instinctively for the Dragoon at his hip and then froze when he recognized Hickok. Although he seemed to know better than to pick a fight with the tall man, he still muttered: 'You got no right interferin' in this, Wild Bill.'

Hickok's response was bleak. 'I see a grown man beatin' on a kid. Hell, I figure I got *every* right. So you listen up, Reese. I know you of old — we *all* do. You're all paw and beller when you think you can get away with it. But somethin' tells me you've met your match in this kid. You hear me? You pick a fight with him — a *fair* fight, I mean — an' it might just be *you* who's left sprawled in the dirt.'

'You can't take that tone with me,' Reese said through puffy lips.

'Oh, I *can*,' Hickok replied with

unnerving certainty. 'See, one way or another, you've about frayed your cinch around here, Reese. So you tread real careful from now on, 'cause no one'll cry if me or that boy send you packin'.'

'The hell you say!'

'The hell I say,' Hickok confirmed coldly. 'And while I got your attention, you remember this, too — from now on, the boy's under my protection. Any harm comes to him that I think *you* might be mixed up in and I'll find you an' shoot you down like the cur you are. And if that sticks in your craw, you can take it up with me right now.'

He waited for a few moments. Then:

'No? All right. You been warned, Reese. Mind your manners from now on an' *stay* warned.' Straightening up, he turned to Will, his whole demeanor changing. 'Come on, son,' he said congenially. 'We'll share a fire.'

As they walked off to find their own spot, Will said: 'Thanks for taking up for me, uh . . . Wild Bill.'

'More'n welcome, son. You're new

here, aint you?' he added. 'Don't recall seeing you with this crew before.'

'Joined it the day we left Leavenworth.'

'Runaway, are you?'

'No, sir! It's just . . . my folks need the money real bad.'

'So what did you do to rile your friend Reese, there?'

'My pa was Free State.'

'Well, that's as good a reason as any, I guess, leastways as far as Reese's concerned. But take a piece of advice, kid. I'll watch out for you any way I can. But you made a bad enemy back there. Best you watch *yourself* from here to Utah.'

'I thank you for that, Mr. Hickok,' Will replied. 'I'll be sure an' do jus' that.'

12

Hickok was as good as his word. Over the next week or so, and always in addition to his regular scouting duties, he took it upon himself to watch out for Will. Knowing as much, Reese wisely kept his distance. But Will knew that sooner or later, there would be a reckoning between them. He just wished he shared Hickok's confidence when it came to predicting the winner.

But late one afternoon, he learned that there were other dangers to watch out for, aside from Reese. He was riding drag, as usual, when he thought he heard several gunshots in the far distance. The moving herd was making so much noise that he couldn't be sure.

By the time he'd convinced himself that he'd imagined it, he clearly heard another sound, this time one like thunder.

He looked up, but the sky was cloudless. It was puzzling.

'*Will!*'

Twisting around, he saw Ira Thomas about seventy feet away, on the far side of a shifting curtain of dust. Ira had been riding flank, but had pulled back for some reason. When Will saw the amiable cowboy jabbing a finger urgently toward the north, he realized why.

A brown tide was flowing down over a rise about half a mile away, headed in their direction.

'*Buffalo!*' yelled Thomas.

Will froze at the sight. The herd was so large it was impossible to estimate its size. It poured down the hill toward the flats, looking more like a mudslide from this distance, and there seemed to be no end to it. The buffalo were following their leaders . . . who were headed straight at the flank of the slow-moving cattle.

Right then Parsons came out of nowhere, drew alongside Thomas and the two held a hurried conversation. Still the buffalo raced down the slope, each animal turned on a slight angle as it came, and all of them flattening the long grass before them.

Enormous creatures with boundless energy, they ran with their massive, shaggy heads down, broad bulky shoulders heaving as they moved with the speed of a good horse. There were bulls that measured an easy six feet to the shoulder, golden-colored calves scurrying after their mothers, and feisty younger males competing with each other as if this were more of a race than a stampede. And even with their lighter-weight, lighter-brown summer coats, the adults of both sexes were uniformly gigantic.

The ground under Will's horse began to tremble and he had to tighten rein to keep the skittish animal under control. Meanwhile, Parsons and Thomas broke away from the cattle and started galloping across the plain, as if going to meet the oncoming buffalo. Although he had no idea what they intended to do, Will turned Prince and rode after them, knowing only that he had to do something to help avert almost certain disaster.

No sooner had he broken clear of the herd than another rider came galloping out of the dust — Reese. Their two horses almost collided, but each rider reacted quickly and drew rein in time. Sitting stirrup to stirrup, they stared at each other for one charged moment. As usual, Reese's blue eyes were filled with animosity.

'*Get back to the herd!*' he yelled.

But Will had already made up his mind what he was going to do, and nothing Reese said was going to make him change it. Whipping Prince with the reins, he yelled, '*Yaaahhh!*' and then raced after Parsons and Thomas.

Cursing, Reese spurred his horse after Will.

By now, Parsons and Thomas had ridden around the oncoming buffalo, then turned their horses so that they could ride back alongside them, each man dragging his slicker from where it was tied behind his cantle. Spurring his horse, Parsons surged up toward the leaders and started waving the slicker over his head and screaming himself hoarse.

Still galloping out to meet them, Will realized that they were trying to make the leading buffalo change direction. In that same moment he understood something else, too: that because a buffalo's eyes were located on the side of its skull, its forward vision was severely limited. That's why they were running with their bodies at an angle — so they could better see where they were going.

Reese now overtook him. Joining his companions, he turned his mount and started flapping his hat wildly back and forth in an effort to force the buffalo onto a course that would avoid the herd. Will followed suit, turning his own horse nimbly when he drew parallel to the running buffalo and then riding in as close as he dared, yelling and waving his own freed blanket for all he was worth.

This close to the herd, the sound was deafening. Hooves drummed without let-up, each lurching stride accompanied by an unsettling, pig-like grunt that sounded like a dog's warning growl.

As Will guided Prince in as close as he dared to the charging buffalo, he stared at the creatures in wonderment. Their eyes were wide, their nostrils distended, their lips curled back over teeth the size of dominos. The herd stank, too — of dirt and urine, dung and sweat.

Looking beyond Reese, then Thomas, then Parsons, Will saw that the distance between the buffalo and the cattle was closing rapidly. He could also tell that the cattle were starting to spook and break ranks as they sensed the oncoming threat. But as best Will could see from his speeding horse, the buffalo leaders were gradually turning. There might be a chance to avoid a collision yet.

Then, without warning, Ira Thomas's horse stumbled.

Will thought: *Prairie dog hole.*

The animal pitched over in a bizarre kind of somersault, and when it came down again Ira was beneath it, crushed by a twelve hundred pounds of horse-flesh.

Will was horrified, but right then there was no time to mourn. Ahead, Reese curved his horse around the broken remnants of the man and his mount, and kept going with hardly a break in stride.

Then it was Will's turn. Knowing he could never handle a horse as well as Reese, he allowed his mount to leap the obstacle instead.

Prince cleared the tangle but landed awkwardly and crashed into one of the buffalo. Will yelped as pain stabbed the leg that was caught between the two animals, and for a sickening moment he thought he was going to fall from the saddle and die beneath the buffalos' hooves.

Then Prince recovered from a final stumble and kept running.

Will felt the pain in his leg fade, and guessed that nothing was broken.

'*Haaaa! Haaa!!!*'

Ahead, the buffalo were definitely veering eastward now, taking a new course that, with any luck, would take them behind the cattle herd and not right through it.

Energized by the thought, Will kept screaming at the buffalo to turn and continued to wave his blanket back and forth until the blanket seemed to weigh a ton and he didn't think he could wave it any more.

Then a scattering of additional riders — a frantic glance showed him Simpson, Hickok and some of Simpson's lieutenants — came surging back from the train, waving hats or blankets, slickers or spare shirts, and now there was not a shred of doubt about it — the buffalo were *definitely* curving away from the herd.

Spent, Will angled Prince away from the last of the trailing buffalo and reined in. He was so exhausted he almost fell from the saddle. He felt sick from the wild run and the memory of what had happened to Ira Thomas. He bent at the waist, sucked in great, greedy draughts of air, and when he looked up again he saw Parsons and Reese about thirty yards away. They had also quit the run to let the newcomers take over and continue hazing the buffalo onto their new course.

Will ran a forearm across his sweated brow. He felt Reese's eyes on him, but ignoring him he turned and remounted, then walked Prince back along the great churned gouge that marked the buffalos' passage, until he came to the dead horse and its rider.

He dismounted and tossed his blanket over what was left of Ira Thomas. Then, taking off his hat, he bowed his head and muttered a few words over the body.

Parsons and Reese rode up and swung down to join him.

'You all right, sprout?' asked the trailboss, his voice gravelly and subdued.

Not trusting himself to speak, Will only nodded.

'You make sure you get that leg seen to by Cheater, you hear?'

Not understanding what Parsons meant, Will frowned. But when he looked down and saw that several knots of coarse brown buffalo hair had caught in the seam of his pants-leg, he realized just how close he'd come to having the leg crushed between the buffalo and his horse.

Before Will could respond, Reese snapped: 'Who's that?'

Three strangers were walking their horses over the rise about fifty yards away, following the trail of devastation the buffalo had left in their wake. All three were in their early thirties and one of them was leading a packhorse.

Curious, Parsons walked wearily up the incline to meet them, Reese plodding along behind him. A moment later Will joined them, limping slightly.

The newcomers shortened rein. They all favored battered felt hats and oilcloth dusters over flannel shirts and corduroy or canvas pants. One of them, a burly man with a heavy brown beard, whistled softly when he saw the now-distant buffalo herd.

'Whoo-ee!' he said. 'Them wisents are like to run from here to sundown.' Then he grinned, showing teeth stained brown by a lifetime's addiction to Little Katie chewing tobacco. 'Purebright's the name, friend, Oscar Purebright. And these two rascals is my friends, Jacob Rice and Terry O'Dowd. We're headin' for California: aim to make us a fortune in the goldfields.'

His accent told them he was from the East, possibly Ohio or Pennsylvania.

Having made introductions, he glanced back at his companions and said: 'Well, I do humbly apologize, boys. Don't look like we're gonna get to eat them buffalo steaks after all.'

Reese scowled. 'What does that mean?' he asked softly.

Purebright faced front again. 'It means we figured to pick off one o' them there critters and have us a couple of juicy steaks for our supper. I swear I hit one of them wisents at least three times, but the damn thing just wouldn't fall down.'

Will thought: *I was right, then. I did hear gunshots just before the stampede.*

'That the weapon you used to shoot it?' asked Reese, indicating the squirrel rifle resting across Purebright's lap.

'Ayuh.'

'What caliber?'

'Thirty-two,' Purebright replied proudly.

'Then you're even dumber than you look, mister,' growled Reese.

He grabbed Purebright and yanked him out of his saddle. Purebright lost his grip on the rifle and hit the ground hard. The thin-faced, squint-eyed man Purebright had introduced as Jacob Rice grabbed for the little pocket revolver tucked in his sash, but Parsons was way ahead of him, drawing and cocking his own gun to freeze Rice where he was.

Reese now dragged Purebright back down the slope until they came to the corpse of the horse and the blanket-draped body of Ira Thomas. There, he shoved Purebright so hard, he fell to his knees in the freshly churned dirt.

'A thirty-two caliber bullet wouldn't do more'n *tickle* a critter like a buffalo,' Reese said angrily. 'All you did was spook that herd an' get a good man killed.'

Furious, Purebright scrambled back up. 'That herd was as peaceful as Sunday mornin', mister! How was I to know it'd end up runnin'?'

'Likely it wouldn't've, if you'd used the right tool for the job,' Reese replied. 'If you'd used a heavier cartridge you wouldn't had to keep bustin' off one cap after another until you spooked 'em. Out here in the middle of no place, a man's supposed to know things like that if he aims to survive.'

'Now listen here,' said Purebright, bristling, 'I'm sorry for what happened to your friend, but it weren't no fault o' mine.'

Reese didn't see it that way. He drew back his fist, intending to belt Purebright, but Parsons stopped him.

Hurrying up to him, he yelled: '*Reese! Enough!*'

Reese looked into Purebright's face. It showed fear now, and Reese grudgingly realized that Parsons was right. He was a greenhorn: he couldn't possibly have foreseen that his stupidity would end up the way it had. But without anyone to take his frustration out on, he only felt Ira's death all the keener.

'I reckon — ' he began.

'*Reese!*'

This time it was Will who called his name and hearing the urgency in the single word, the broken-nosed cowboy reacted instinctively. He turned and dropped to a crouch, his gun jumping into his hand. The Dragoon blasted once and Jacob Rice hunched up, dropped the gun Will had seen him draw, and slumped over his horse's neck.

'Damnation!' cried Purebright. 'What'd you have to do that for?'

The third man, Terry O'Dowd, urged his horse alongside that of Rice and made a quick inspection of the wound.

'He's been hit in the arm,' he reported over Rice's wail.

Parsons spat angrily. 'Put that gun down, Lyle! And you, Purebright — catch up your horse an' fetch your man down to the herd with us. I'll have our cook patch him up.'

Purebright glared at him. 'Don't bother, mister. We can take care of our own.'

'That,' said Parsons, 'I *seriously* doubt. But the offer's there. Up to you whether or not you take it.' He turned to Reese and Will, dismissing the greenhorn with the gesture. 'Come on, you two. We got a friend to bury.'

13

Purebright and O'Dowd rode out with Jacob Rice between them. He was barely conscious and facing the kind of rough-and-ready surgery that would be more likely to kill him than cure him. Watching them go, Will told himself that Reese had been right — if a man wanted to survive in the wilderness, he had better learn his business and learn it fast.

As for Reese himself . . . if he felt he owed Will any thanks for warning him before Rice could shoot him, he kept it well hidden. Silently they wrapped Ira Thomas in his blanket and buried him where he'd fallen and hoped that his grave wouldn't be disturbed by scavengers after the sun went down.

Fortunately Will's leg, which had been badly bruised, healed quickly. As a result, the next few days passed in their usual fashion: rising before dawn, riding drag, eating dust and falling into his blankets at night, totally exhausted, to sleep the sleep of the dead until the sun came up and it was time to do it all over again.

The worst part, he discovered, was riding nighthawk. With the herd bedded down and the silence broken only by the yipping coyotes, there was too much time to think. How was his mother? Was she even still *alive?* How were Julia and Eliza, Helen, May and baby Charles?

It was then that the homesickness was at its worst, and more than once, while he circled the herd, making sure all was well, his bottom lip would twitch uncontrollably.

As if sensing his misery, Wild Bill never missed a chance to seek him out and educate him about the plains and the outdoor life. Will listened avidly, soaking up all the knowledge he could, partly because it was a distraction at a time when he really needed it, but mostly because he was convinced that a man or even a boy, as he still was could never have enough learning.

Early one evening they were talking over a supper of beef stew when Hickok suddenly sat up straight and said: 'Riders comin' in.'

He set his plate aside and got to his feet, his movements as fluid as always, his long-fingered hands hanging loose at his sides, ready to grab for his distinctive Colts the minute he sensed trouble. But after a moment he relaxed and gestured toward the two riders that Will now saw coming in off the night-dark plains.

'It's Gabe an' Kit,' Hickok murmured.

'You know 'em?'

'Yup. And so should *you*, Will. That there's Jim Bridger, an' right beside him, Kit Carson.'

Will sucked in a breath. '*What?* You're funnin' me, ain't you?'

'It's them, all right.'

A few minutes later the buckskin-clad newcomers came into the circle of firelight, riding slow and comfortable. The flames showed Will faces that were as etched and weathered as the trails they'd blazed.

'Light and set, fellers!' called Hickok, meeting with his hand extended. 'Will — pour these here miscreants some coffee, will you? They look like they could use it.'

Carson, or Christopher Houston Carson to give him his full name, was a plain-looking man with dark, curly hair that spilled from beneath a well-worn beaver hat. His face was wide, his cheekbones high, his skin surprisingly pale and his manner warm as he pumped Hickok's hand. He was in his middle or late forties, as near as Will could judge.

But it was hard for him to credit that such an ordinary-looking man could have led such an extraordinary life. By all accounts, Carson had run away from home when he was sixteen so that he could trap fur in the Rocky Mountains. He'd also scouted Mexican California and was known as a first-class wilderness guide and all-round fighting man. A veteran of the Mexican-American War, he knew Indians, too, as well as any white man was ever likely to. In his time he'd married into the Arapaho and Cheyenne tribes, and also worked as an Indian agent with the Apaches.

Bridger, by contrast, was a few years older: a big, powerful-looking man who resembled the Indians among whom he, too, had so often lived. His hair was fair, his blue eyes set close together, his mouth a firm, determined line. Looking at him, Will sensed there was nothing Bridger couldn't do, and do well. He spoke a number of Indian dialects, as well as French and Spanish. And like Carson, he too was a squaw man. His first wife, a Flathead, had died in childbirth. Subsequently he had married the daughter of a Shoshone chief. A respected explorer, trapper and pathfinder, his fame was such that Bridger's Pass had been named after him.

The three men exchanged greetings, and then Hickok indicated Will. 'This here is my associate, Master William Cody. He's a boy who shows promise.'

'He does, eh?' said Bridger, offering one big, callused hand. 'Put 'er there, son.'

'Go grab yourself some vittles,' said Hickok, returning to the fire. 'Then we'll yarn a while.'

'Will do,' said Carson. 'But we're only stoppin' for the night. We got business in Utah.'

'So've we,' said Hickok. 'Runnin' supplies out to the Utah Expedition.'

'Johnston's army?' asked Bridger, swapping a glance with Carson. 'That explains it, then.'

'Explains what?'

'Why the Mormons are so damn' keen to buy my fort,' said Bridger. 'Looks like they're settlin' in for the long haul.'

That night, after the other men had turned in, Will sat listening to Hickok, Bridger and Carson swap stories — or yarns, as they called them. Eventually the conversation turned to the plains, the enormity and beauty of which Will still hadn't gotten over.

'You think this is special,' said Bridger, 'you don't know the half of it, young William. Mountains polishin' the sun, rivers burstin' with fish, trails untrod 'cept by Injuns 'n' wild things, an' forests so quiet 'n' still it's like watchin' a first snow. An' holier than any church the Good Lord had in mind.'

It was clearly a subject to which Carson had also given considerable thought. 'Lord, there was a time, and not too far back, either, when a man could ride moon to moon an' never see another soul.'

'Wish I'd seen it,' murmured Will.

'You can,' said Bridger. 'But you'd better get a hurry on. It's vanishin' by the day.'

'That'll never happen, surely?'

'It's *already* happenin', young fella. Greenhorns headin' west, thicker'n ticks on a short dog, and all of 'em too busy takin' an' ownin' to really see it an' care for it. See, the Injun, he lives *with* life, William. He don't try to scalp it flat, like us whites.'

Carson took another gulp of his coffee. ''Course, it was different when I was your age,' he said. 'Jest the findin' an' seein' was the whole of it, then leavin' everythin' jus' like it was . . . untouched.'

'Can it be saved, Mr. Bridger?' asked Will. 'I mean, before it disappears altogether?'

'Possible. If the white man took to the natural way of things, like the Injun.'

'There ain't much chance o' *that*,' muttered Hickok. 'But this I promise you, Will — the nearest thing your kids'll ever get to the land as it is right now is you tellin' 'em how it was.'

'As you say,' said Carson. 'But don't be too downcast, boy. You're one of the lucky ones, born while she's still there. Now all you got to do is make the most of it.'

★ ★ ★

Will was still thinking about the wide-open spaces when, a few days later, Parsons rode up alongside him. 'Sprout!'

'Yessir!'

'Go tell Mr. Simpson we got company.'

Will looked at him above the line of his drag-dusted bandanna. 'Company, Mr. Parsons?'

Parsons hooked a thumb to the northwest. 'Cheyennes. About a dozen or more. They been doggin' us for the past twenty minutes an' they're makin' me itch somethin' fierce.'

Will immediately looked in that direction but could see nothing through the haze. 'Yessir!'

He turned his horse and galloped around the herd. Reese, who was riding flank, glanced over one shoulder, saw him coming and swiftly moved to intercept him.

'Runnin' out on us, kid?' he called.

162

But there was no longer the malice in him that there had been earlier; since Ira Thomas's death, his attitude toward Will had changed subtly.

Will, not picking up on that, had neither the time nor the inclination to reply. He rode around Reese and spurred his horse past the herd and on, past the line of equally slow-moving Conestogas until he reached the head of the train, where Simpson and Hickok were riding side by side.

Both men turned as Will reined up alongside them.

'Indians, Mr. Simpson!' Will reported breathlessly. 'Cheyennes, Mr. Parsons says. They been trailin' us for twenty minutes.'

Simpson and Hickok swapped looks. Simpson scratched thoughtfully at his tobacco-stained beard. 'How many?'

'Dozen. Maybe more.'

'Wearin' paint?'

'He didn't say.'

'So let's go find out,' said Hickok. Telling the drivers of the first wagons in line to keep moving, Simpson led the way back along the trail until the dust thinned and they saw Parsons sitting his horse beside the stalled chuck wagon. Reese was there, too, leaning forward with his arms crossed over the pommel of his saddle.

As the newcomers drew rein, Reese looked at Will and said: 'Figured you was lightin' out.'

'And you couldn't wait to tell Mr. Parsons here, is that it?' Will retorted.

Reese shrugged and turned back to the Indians.

The small band of Cheyenne were spread out along a grassy ridge a quarter-mile away. Will felt an instinctive surge of fear, for aside from the Kickapoo Indians back home, these were the first Indians he'd ever seen.

They wore breechcloths and leggings, and fringed buckskin shirts adorned with lazy-stitch beadwork. A number of them carried colorful, feather-hung war shields. Long, eagle-feather war bonnets fluttered in the keen wind. They

164

were armed with lances, old rifles and short bows, jawbone clubs, hatchets and even horsewhips.

'How do we play this?' asked Parsons.

'We see what they want,' said Hickok.

'They want the cattle, don't they?' asked Will.

'Maybe,' allowed Hickok. 'Or more likely they just need a little sweet-talkin' to let us pass.'

Will wasn't sure he grasped what Hickok meant, but this was no time for questions. All he could do now was watch with a nagging sense of fear as Hickok rode out to meet the Indians. Although he feared that his friend was riding to his death, there were no war-cries, no shots or fired arrows.

When Hickok was close enough, he held up his right hand in the accepted, palm-out sign of peace. To his relief, the Cheyenne replied in kind. Then, wrapping his reins around his saddle horn, Wild Bill began to gesture with his hands.

'What's he doin'?' Will asked quietly.

It was Cheater Webb who replied. '*Wibluto*,' said the cook. 'Sign language. Good way to talk, when neither of you knows the other fella's tongue.'

The conversation went on for what seemed like forever. Then Hickok nodded, unwound his reins and started his horse back to the stalled wagon at a canter.

'Well?' asked Simpson when Hickok reined up.

'There ain't one of 'em older'n eighteen, nineteen,' Hickok reported tersely. 'An' they're lookin' for glory. I offered 'em ten head of cattle in return for safe passage. They asked for fifty. I said maybe we could run to twenty. Lead buck said that wasn't enough and upped it to sixty. Plus horses — half of your stock, Parsons.'

Parsons spat to one side. 'That'll be a cold day in summer.'

'He knows that,' Hickok replied. 'He's pushin' us, 'cause the thing him and his friends want more'n anythin' right now is to count *coup*.'

Will, having heard the expression before, knew it meant that a warrior could prove his courage and earn status within his tribe by touching his enemy during combat.

'Maybe they're bluffin',' suggested Cheater.

Reese made a dismissive sound in his throat and shook his head. 'One thing you better know about Indians,' he said. 'When they give their word, you can build a statue on it. These fellas ain't bluffin'.'

'So they'll come with blood in their eyes whether we give in to 'em or not?'

'About the size of it,' said Wild Bill.

The wagon-master turned to watch the herd vanishing into its own dust. 'Then let 'em come,' he decided grimly. 'We fight 'em here and we *stop* 'em here. If we don't, and they get anywhere near the herd, we got a stampede on our hands.'

'Hell, there's fifteen of them sons-abitches!' said Cheater.

'I grant you they're long odds,' said Simpson. 'But we're better-armed and we got decent cover.' He swung around to Will. 'Ride on up the train, boy, find one of my lieutenants an' tell 'em we need a few good men back here, *pronto*.'

Will was about to nod when Reese barked: 'Too damn' late for that.' And then: 'Here they come!'

14

Eager for glory, the Cheyennes charged down off the ridge, spreading out as they came and yelling war cries.

Simpson snapped: 'All right — it's been settled for us! Cheater, grab your Colt. You got anythin' in the wagon the boy can use?'

'A rifle,' Cheater replied, and went to get it.

'You had any experience with rifles, boy?' asked Simpson, unlimbering his own Model '55s.

'Yes, sir,' said Will.

'Then don't let us down, kid,' called Reese, dropping to one knee. 'You do that an' I'll shoot you myself.'

Will was about to reply when Reese winked to show that he was only joking.

He actually *winked*.

Then Cheater came back from the chuck wagon and thrust a Mississippi

Yaeger rifle into Will's hands, along with a powder horn and a pouch of .58 caliber balls.

Hurriedly Will tried to familiarize himself with the muzzle-loader, but there wasn't time. For one thing he was so scared that it was hard to concentrate. For another —

Sky-blue arrows started zipping through the air, sticking into the chuck wagon's canvas or thudding hard into its water barrel and sideboards. Will hefted the rifle, hauled back the hammer, watched the Cheyenne over the V-notch front sight and wondered if he would live through the next few minutes.

'Stand your ground, everyone!' called Hickok. 'Let them come into range and then don't miss a shot.'

Closer . . . closer . . . and all the while their war cries growing louder . . . louder . . .

Calm as a poet, Hickok drew his own matched .36s and carefully took aim.

'*Now!*'

Every man fired at once.

The fusillade made Will flinch so hard he almost lost grip on the rifle. But he quickly regained control of himself and teeth clenched, took aim and fired. The old percussion rifle boomed and more by luck than design, the ball knocked a charging Cheyenne's horse out from under him.

To either side of Will, Simpson, Parsons, Reese and Cheater continued pouring fire at the oncoming Indians. The Cheyenne Will had just unhorsed leapt back to his feet, waving a feathered lance defiantly. A second later his head vanished in a crimson cloud and he fell backward with his legs kicking.

Trying to block out everything around him, Will knelt and focused on reloading. With no accurate way to calculate the amount of black powder he needed, he placed a ball in the palm of his hand and then measured out enough of a charge to cover it. Fishing the ball from the mound, he dropped the powder down the barrel. Next, he took a patch from the pouch, chewed it briefly to soften and lubricate it, then tucked the ball into and finally tamped the two home with the ramrod.

Dragging back the hammer, he was ready to fire again.

Suddenly Cheater yelped and swore. Will saw he'd taken an arrow in the side, above his hipbone, and was now slumped back against one of the wagon-wheels.

Will faced front again, felt a moment of horror at just how close the Indians had gotten then calmed himself, chose a target, aimed and pulled the trigger.

A face-painted brave was knocked from his horse and started screaming his death chant. Parsons thumbed back the hammer on his Walker Colt and finished him off.

Will broke ranks and ran to the cook. Cheater Webb's jowly face was sweaty and bloodless, but when he saw the boy coming he shook his head and called: 'I'll live!'

Then gritting his teeth, he continued

to aim and fire at the oncoming Cheyennes.

Will dropped to one knee and reloaded again. Behind him the team-horses kept fussing in the traces and trying to drag the wheel-locked wagon away. He fired again, missed and swore — he'd heard plenty of that over the past few weeks, despite the oath Alexander Majors made his employees take. Then he was reloading again, as Wild Bill stood tall beside him, calmly firing one Colt, then the other, into the enemy.

Reese dropped another Indian, who flew backward off his horse's rump and fell dead in the long grass. Caught up in the heat of battle, Simpson actually went forward with both Model '55s belching smoke ahead of him. A Cheyenne came charging at him. He fired an ancient pistol at the wagon-master, but missed. Simpson returned fire from both weapons and two bullets cored the Indian from belly to back-bone and smacked him from his saddle.

Hit hard, the Cheyennes stopped their charge and began riding back and forth, screaming insults and challenges. Grimly Will reloaded the Mississippi-Yaeger, working faster than ever now as he grew more familiar with the procedure. Glancing hurriedly along the line, he saw Reese watching him.

'You still here, boy?'

'Looks like it,' Will replied.

Reese threw him a tight smile. 'Good for you.'

Then he faced front again as the Cheyennes launched another charge.

One brave rushed in closer than the rest and before Simpson could do anything about it, slammed his jawbone club down on the wagon-master's head. Simpson's felt hat absorbed most of the blow but still the wagon-master went down in a heap.

Enraged, Parsons broke ranks and shot the Indian point-blank. The brave toppled from his horse with half his jaw missing. He then rolled back and forth with one leg kicking spastically until, at last, the leg went still.

Parsons bent to drag Simpson back toward the wagon, then dropped to one knee as an arrow skewered his left leg. Will drew a bead on a lance-carrying Indian whose face was covered in red and yellow paint. With no time to aim, he simply pointed the rifle and pulled the trigger. The bullet clipped the Indian's shoulder and his horse reared up and unseated him.

'You're doin' okay!' called Reese.

Will tipped his hat in acknowledgement and started reloading.

Hickok shot another Indian off his horse. Will saw the look of shock on the brave's face as a hole appeared between his eyes and blood shot out the back of his head.

Will had never seen anything so hideous, and it froze him in his tracks.

'*Kid!*'

Will recognized Reese's voice. It jolted him back to reality. He saw that the Cheyenne he'd hit in the shoulder was back on his feet. The brave had snatched up his lance and was preparing to hurl it at him.

Reese hurled himself into Will, knocking him out of the way just as the lance left the Cheyenne's hand. An instant later it punched Reese right through the chest. He fired one reflexive shot into the ground and then collapsed.

Will was too shocked to do anything but allow instinct to dictate his actions. He aimed from the hip and shot the Cheyenne in the chest. The ball shattered the Indian's bone-and-bead breastplate and did pretty much the same to the sternum beneath it.

Will quickly tried to reload the rifle with fumbling hands. He spilled more powder than he caught in his palm and swore again, mad at himself.

Concentrate . . . concentrate . . .

But Reese —

Don't think about that, not now . . .

Then a shadow fell across him and a hand came to rest on his shoulder.

'It's all right, Will,' said Hickok. 'It's over.'

Blinking, Will looked at Wild's Bill's long face.

'W-What?'

'It's *over*,' Hickok repeated.

It was a moment more before the words sunk in. Then Will looked around as if coming out of a daze. The three surviving Cheyenne warriors were riding back over the far ridge. The grass between Will and the fleeing Indians was littered with the bodies of their dead brothers and dead and dying horses.

Nearby, lay the body of a single white man.

Reese.

Will felt an overwhelming urge to sob, but swallowed the sound. 'H-He saved my life,' he managed to say after a moment.

'Looks that way,' Hickok said.

'But . . . he *hated* me.'

'No,' said Hickok, crouching beside him and putting an arm about Will's shoulders. 'He hated what he *thought* you was. When you got the chance to show your true metal, that you was more than just a kid, a *passenger* . . . I reckon he saw his mistake, an' figgered you was worth savin'.'

Will looked down at his boots, wishing he could stop his hands from shaking. 'He died for me,' he said quietly, his voice puzzled, as if he found it impossible to believe. 'And I can't even *thank* him.'

'That's where you're wrong,' said Hickok. 'He just give you a chance he himself didn't get. You can thank him by not wastin' it.'

'How do I do that?' asked Will.

'By makin' yourself count,' said Hickok. 'You got great things ahead of you, Will. I knew it the minute I first clapped eyes on you, and likely Reese came to see as much for himself. There's nothin' you can't achieve, boy — *if* 'you got the guts to take every opportunity life gives you.'

He glanced over his shoulder. Simpson was sitting up and rubbing his sore head. Cheater Webb and Parsons were both favoring their arrow wounds.

'Now,' Hickok said, gesturing to their horses. 'Enough yammer. Go fetch help back here, *pronto*, while I wrap Reese in his blanket an' get him ready for a Christian burial.'

Part Four — Pony Express Rider

15

Simpson, Parsons and Cheater Webb all had their wounds tended and were advised to rest up for a few days. They managed a little less than twenty-four hours. Then, almost as one, they insisted on getting back to their respective duties and to hell with the discomfort.

But in its way, the battle left scars on Will, too. As the supply train pushed on into Colorado Territory, he felt a confusing sense of loss at Reese's death. He couldn't say that he'd liked the man: he hadn't. But toward the end, he felt there might have been a chance for friendship had Reese lived.

But Reese *hadn't* lived.

He'd died so that *Will* could live.

And the guilt Will felt over that also changed him.

Before they buried Reese, Wild Bill

presented Will with the man's Dragoon Colt and weapons belt. 'Here,' he said. 'Can't bring myself to throw dirt on a piece of artillery as fine as this.'

Will shook his head. 'I can't take that.'

'Reese doesn't have any more use for it,' Hickok pointed out. 'But *you* just might, if you go on to live the kinda life I think you will.'

Will had no idea what he meant by that, but he stowed the belt with the rest of his gear and took to carrying the big Dragoon in his waistband. Although Wild Bill taught him how to shoot with it, he had no call to use it after the Cheyenne attack.

Though plagued by headaches following his injury, Lew Simpson pushed everyone as hard as he dared, and somehow Colorado came and went and the vast, dry country of Utah opened up before them. Two and a half months of hard travel had finally brought the supply train to its destination.

And Will was out of work.

When he finally returned home, it was to find his mother still weak but in better health than when he'd left. And though it had only been a matter of months, the rest of the family looked so much older as they lined up to greet him — especially young Charles, who had now taken on a definite identity of his own.

But that particular trail ran both ways. Will's family saw an enormous change in *him*, too. On the long journey back from Utah, he'd spent some time at the old military post of Fort Laramie, where almost four thousand Sioux, Cheyenne and Arapaho were more or less permanently encamped. It was there that he renewed his acquaintance with Kit Carson and Jim Bridger, as well as a number of other celebrated hunters, trappers and Indian fighters. It was also there that he decided that he wanted to spend the rest of his life as they did — as a plainsman.

He sat for hours and watched them talk to the Indians in *Wibluto*. Without the need for a single spoken word, they could hold long and often surprisingly complex conversations. In addition to sign, he made it a point to pick up a passable knowledge of Sioux from the local Indians.

It was hardly surprising, then, that he found life in Salt Creek Valley tame and predictable by comparison and though he stuck with it, he still yearned for the great open plains.

When he turned fifteen, he decided he could stand it no more. In need of a job, he hoped that Alexander Majors, of Russell, Majors & Waddell, might again provide it.

He'd heard that the three businessmen were about to launch a mail-transportation system that promised to beat the twenty-five day target of the Butterfield Overland Mail by fifteen days or more. This messenger service was to be run under the auspices of the newly formed Central Overland and Pike's Peak Express Company, and would stretch from St. Joseph, Missouri, to Sacramento, California; a route of two thousand miles that would encompass two ranges of mountains as well as great stretches of plain and alkali desert.

One fine March morning, Will rode out to Majors' antebellum house on the hinges of Kansas City and was fortunate enough to find the businessman at home. As bullish and well-groomed as ever, Majors was pleased to see his young protege again. After a hearty handshake, he studied the lanky boy in patched buckskins for a long time before finally nodding his approval.

'You've grown some since I last saw you,' he said, 'but you're still light enough, I reckon.'

'Light enough, sir?'

'Yes. Weight is a priority. To meet our obligations, you'll have to cover fifteen miles an hour, every hour you're in the saddle. No time for pausing to gawp at the scenery, or swap talk with anyone you meet along the way.'

'That suits me,' said Will.

'Your wages will be fifty dollars a

month. But the better you ride, the more you'll make. Even so, you'll earn every penny. You'll take the mail and *literally* guard it with your life. You'll ride like the wind along a route some forty-five miles in length, stopping only long enough at each of our stations to change horses, and you'll do it every day of the week. Think you can handle it?'

'I reckon.'

Satisfied, Majors face suddenly clouded. 'You've heard the rumors, of course?'

'About the coming war, you mean?'

That was *exactly* what Majors meant. A Republican politician by the name of Abraham Lincoln was running for the presidency, and had promised to ban slavery in all U.S. Territories should he be elected. Seven southern states, whose cotton-based economies relied on slavery, saw any attempt to change their way of life as a violation of their rights, and were already promising to fight tooth and nail if Lincoln tried to make good on his pledge.

'It'll be a hell of a thing, Master Cody, if what I suspect and fear really comes to pass,' Majors confided. 'Brother against brother . . . a hell of a thing. But the side most able to communicate speedily and effectively will be the winner. And in the long term, that's the service we aim to provide. We'll only carry messages written on the thinnest paper,' he continued. 'You'll carry them in a *mochila* — that's a kind of waterproof pouch — slung under your arm. And remember, lad — you'll keep your own weight to the minimum. We've no call for skeletons, but neither do we have any need for boys who carry extra pounds on them, or wear more clothes than is necessary. Still game?'

'Yes, sir.'

Majors thrust out one hand. 'Then welcome to the Pony Express, Master Cody. I think it's a job that will suit you perfectly.'

★　★　★

One week later, as Will concentrated on the lonely trail ahead, he remembered reporting to the company's impressive, redbrick stables in St Joe and taking a shine to one horse in particular — the fine California roan he was riding right now. Neither had he been mistaken in his choice of horseflesh.

At first, as he carried the mail from Rocky Ridge to Three Crossings, he enjoyed the scenery. The countryside was as beautiful as it was vast, the rolling plains broken only occasionally by low wooded hills. The weather was also heating up, despite being only spring, and for as far as Will could see the sky was a cloudless zenith blue.

But the plainsman in him had already spotted what could be big trouble ahead for the territory. The leaves on the trees — mostly bur oak, post oak, hackberry and persimmon — hung loose and lifeless, and their color seemed somehow faded, the tips edged with the faintest, ragged brown fringe. There were also signs of dieback, too, in the crowns of those same trees — branches devoid of any foliage at all, rising skyward from the rest of the canopy like bony fingers.

They foretold a drought the likes of which had never been seen before.

It could be that he was mistaken. He could only hope so. But in any case, his was no job for a lollygagger. A man had to have his wits about him if he were to ride at full speed through a land that still offered a wide range of unpleasant surprises.

There was no shortage of Indians in the territory. Arapaho and Cheyenne, Pawnee and Comanche, Kansa, Kiowa and Osage were everywhere. Worse, they were, as Jim Bridger had once told him, all notional in their disposition: meaning they could change from friend to foe in an instant. The territory also had more than its share of bad men left over from the border wars of the mid- to late-1850s.

Still, not all the surprises that awaited him were bad. One afternoon he spotted a great cloud of dust smudging the northern sky. He feared that he might be in for a storm, though it hardly seemed likely, since the drought he had feared seemed to be coming to pass. He left the trail and headed for a ridge a quarter-mile away to take a better look.

Inherently cautious, he shortened rein and dismounted just before he reached the top. Tethering his horse to some scrub, he removed his hat and crawled the rest of the way to the crest.

What met his gaze on the far side took his breath away.

A massive herd of buffalo sat like a vast, shaggy blanket on the prairie below. Such was its size that he could hardly see where it ended. He guessed there were tens of thousands of them. Calves grazed under the watchful eyes of their mothers, as gigantic bulls flicked their tails to keep the flies at bay and lifted their heads to the sky so that they could smell each other better. Feisty young bulls bellowed challenges at each other, or to impress potential mates. Here a particularly old bull rolled in dust to rid himself of ticks and lice. Others rubbed themselves against the scant few trees to mark their territory. The largest bulls stalked the fringes of the herd, keeping watch on their surroundings, and occasionally lowering and shaking their huge heads threateningly whenever they caught something on the thin breeze they didn't like.

Watching them, Will was temporarily transported back to the stampede that had cost Ira Thomas his life. Looking back on it, he had seemed so young then. Now, if anything, he felt so much older than his years. He wasn't sure if that was a good or bad thing. He just knew it was a fact.

Then his horse shook its head, the tethered reins made the brush rustle, and he remembered his oath — *to be faithful to my duties, and so direct all my acts as to win the confidence of my employers.*

It was time to hit the trail again.

16

But that was the thing about Will: he relished every opportunity to push himself that little bit more — a trait Alexander Majors was quick to exploit.

As the months went by, he found himself riding ever westward to make sure the mail got through. In and around the foothills of the Rockies, and from Red Buttes to Sweetwater in particular, the country grew increasingly dangerous. It was then that he was glad to have the weight of Lyle Reese's Dragoon Colt at his hip.

A little after noon one day he galloped into the home-station at Deer Creek to discover that the rider whose job it was to cover the next leg of the route had been killed in a drunken brawl the night before.

'I-Is there anyone else . . . t-to take his . . . place?' Will gasped.

'Only the one,' replied the station-agent, a big-bellied, bearded man named Wes Campbell. '*You.*'

Having just finished a forty-five mile run, Will looked longingly at the station. It wasn't much — a sod-roofed dugout built against a bluff, with adjoining corrals holding spare mounts — but to Will it represented a hot meal and a passably comfortable cot on which to rest his weary bones.

Seeing him hesitate, Campbell reminded him meaningfully: 'Got your remount waitin' for you right here, kid.'

Will sighed. But knew better than to raise any objections. One way or another, the mail had to get through: it was as simple as that.

Trying to forget how exhausted he was, he swung up into the saddle and spurred away, within moments lost in a cloud of dust.

★ ★ ★

When he galloped into the Platte Bridge home-station three hours and the better part of fifty miles later, Finn Ostberg, the Norwegian agent who ran the place, greeted him with:

'You late, *gutt!*'

Will dismounted while his horse was still moving, at the same time sliding the *mochila* pouch off his shoulder and throwing it over the saddle of the remount Ostberg had prepared for the next leg of the route.

'Landslide in Horseshoe Pass,' Will said. 'Had to take the long way around.' He bit off further explanation, and scowled. 'Where's Pony Bob?'

'*Idioten*,' said Ostberg, rolling his eyes. 'Bust hiss leg.'

He shoved the remount's reins at Will, who for once rebelled.

'Mr. Ostberg, I just rid the better part of a hundred miles!'

'Thiss I know,' Ostberg replied crustily. 'We are workin' on a medal for you.'

'But — '

'Time iss wasting, boy!'

Stifling all kinds of imaginative curses,

Will mounted up and rode on into the growing darkness without another word.

★ ★ ★

Fresh horses were waiting for him at every swing-station he came to, but no relief riders. Swing-stations were smaller, more basic posts that existed solely for the switching of horses. They boasted even less frills than the home-stations, which at least offered a chance to eat and sleep. When Will finally reached the home-station at Red Buttes, he prayed that someone else would be waiting to take over. But once again his hopes were dashed.

The agent at Red Buttes was a grizzled, pipe-smoking widow-woman named Alice Singer. She was waiting for Will with a fresh horse when he rode in.

By now he was so tired he didn't so much dismount as fall out of the saddle.

'Where's Pony Bob?' Mrs. Singer demanded.

'Broke his leg.'

'That's too bad.'

Jelly-legged, Will started to walk to the water trough. Now he stopped and looked back at her. 'What's too bad?' he asked.

'Henry Everett,' she said, naming the rider who was to carry the mail to the next station. 'He quit.'

'What?'

Mrs. Singer took the pipe from her mouth. 'Got caught in a flashflood and almost drowned. Shook him up a mite, and he walked off the job.'

Will's shoulders dropped.

'Sorry, son,' she said sincerely. 'You're all we got twixt here an' Willow Spring.'

He continued on to the trough, where he dunked his head several times. When he felt marginally refreshed, he stumbled back to the waiting remount and wearily pulled himself up across leather.

Meanwhile, Mrs. Singer had gone into the station. Now she reappeared, holding a small gunnysack filled with food. 'Ain't much,' she said as she handed it to him. 'Jes' some cold meat an' bread. But it'll keep your ribs from rattlin'.'

'Thanks, Mrs. Singer.' He kicked up the horse and rode away.

Mrs. Singer watched until he was out of sight, then lumbered back to the cabin, thinking: *Boys into men overnight. Wonder if the country knows how much we owe them . . . ?*

Somehow, she doubted it.

★　★　★

It was almost ten in the morning and Amos Ives, the station-agent at Willow Spring, was getting worried. A cavalry patrol had stopped by late the day before to tell him there had been some Arapaho trouble in the area. Given that the rider from Platte Bridge was now well overdue, he could only assume there must be a connection between the two.

Ives was a tall, unsmiling man who looked older than his fifty years. He'd been part of the original crew that built the stations, and had stayed on afterward to man the one here at Willow Spring. Though he'd been raised to see any sign of affection as weakness, he harbored a soft spot for all the boys who rode this stretch of the country. For the most part they had guts, good humor and no quit in them. They knew their manners, too. So the thought of one of them meeting a grisly death at the hands of some feisty Arapahos was cause for concern.

A young skinny youth, Barney McNair, sat mounted nearby. 'He's late,' he said anxiously.

Ives turned and looked at McNair. 'Don't get panicky, son. He'll be here. Count on it.' Inside, Ives wasn't as confident as he sounded. He also knew McNair was anxious to collect the *mochila* and make a start for Sweetwater. Ives couldn't blame him. McNair would have to ride like hell to make up lost time.

Suddenly McNair's horse started fidgeting and both of them stiffened expectantly. To the east the country was a series of gentle, grassy swells and some scanty timber. Now a lone rider appeared over the crest of one of the low hills, and though he hid it behind his perpetual scowl Ives felt a wave of relief wash through him.

'It's Cody,' said McNair, one hand shielding his eyes from the sun. 'That's odd. He don't usually come out this far.'

'No,' Ives agreed. 'Maybe they got Indian trouble farther down the line, as well.'

That there had been difficulties, Indian or otherwise, became obvious when Will rode into the yard. He was slumped over the neck of his horse, so exhausted that when he tried to dismount, he almost fell out of the saddle.

Ives took the *mochila* and tossed it to McNair. McNair caught it and spurred his horse away in the direction of Sweetwater.

Ives supported Will, who was about

to collapse. 'What the hell happened to you, son? Your horse is fine, but it's you who looks like he's been rode hard an' put up wet.'

Will forced himself to find words. 'No one ... else to ... carry the mail ...'

'Where you rid from, son?'

'Started out from ... Cottonwood ... day before yesterday.'

Ives looked at him in disbelief. '*Cottonwood?* Hell, boy, that's two hundred miles from here!'

'Didn't ... exactly have much ... say in it.'

'You better get yourself on inside,' said Ives, thumbing at the log cabin station. 'There's hot food on the stove. Help yourself while I put your horse away.'

Will didn't have the strength to answer. He watched Ives lead his horse off to the corral and then with great effort stumbled into the cabin.

When Ives joined him ten minutes later, he found Will slumped over the old sawbuck table, snoring softly. Beside him, a plate of stew sent steam up to the rafters. Ives looked at the boy for a moment and thought again: *That's a couple of hundred miles from here.*

He crossed the room, took the blanket off the cot in the far corner and gently draped it around Will's shoulders. 'Place is gettin to be a regular nurse 'n' bottle farm,' he grumbled. 'As if there ain't enough work around here as it is, without havin' to fuss around the likes of *you*. That's why I never took me a woman — 'cause I didn't want no wet-eared young 'uns to fuss with.'

But when Will twitched a little and then snored just a tad louder, he smiled and added: 'Rest well, young Cody. Seems to me you've earned it.'

Part Five — Red Leg

17

Given the demands of the job, it was just as well that the completion of the Overland Telegraph Company in 1861 signaled the end of the Pony Express. From then on, messages were sent and received almost instantly and at a fraction of the cost.

Of course, it meant that Will was once again in need of a job. But employment was the least of his concerns right then. When Abraham Lincoln won the presidency in December 1860 with his promise to abolish slavery, one southern state after another began to secede. South Carolina, Mississippi, Florida, Alabama, Georgia, Louisiana and Texas all fell like dominos. In February 1861, these same states created a separate government that called itself the Confederate States of America. Two months later, Confederate forces fired upon Fort Sumter, the Federal garrison in South Carolina, and demanded the surrender of its occupants. After that, it was official — the country was at war with itself.

It was around this same time that Will received a letter from his sister, Julia. The news was bad. Their mother had suffered a stroke, and Julia didn't think she would recover from it. She urged Will to return home to pay his respects while he still could.

When he finally reached home, he was surprised by how small the Cody house now looked to him. Neither did a warm family reunion await him. With the exception of Julia, his brother and other sisters treated him more like a stranger. He couldn't blame them. His job as a Pony Express rider had lasted nineteen months, and in all he'd been away from home for close to two years. After so much time, they were strangers.

With the awkward greetings over, he climbed the stairs to his mother's bedroom, dreading what he would find.

Mary Ann lay in her bed, the paralysis in her left side having affected her once-pretty face as well, giving it a warped, lopsided appearance.

She hadn't known anything about Julia's letter, or the fact that Will was coming home. When he appeared in the doorway, he wasn't even sure she knew who he was. Then her eyes narrowed, her head tilted a little to one side and with great effort she tried to speak to him. At first her words were so slurred, Will couldn't understand her. But finally, she said: 'W-Will . . . th-that you?'

'Yeah, Ma.'

He bent down and carefully hugged her frail body. She felt light as air in his arms.

'Oh, Will,' she said, tears spilling down her gaunt cheeks. 'You've no idea how I've longed to see you again . . . '

'Well, I'm here, now,' he said, swallowing hard.

They sat in silence for a spell, hands clasped, and then to break the heavy mood, he told her about all the places he'd visited and the things he'd seen. For a while she just listened, and seemed to forget her troubles. Once or twice he even managed to make her laugh, by exaggerating some otherwise-ordinary event or other.

But then she asked the question she'd wanted to ask from the moment she'd seen him, first forming each word carefully so that he would understand it.

'How long you home for this time, Will?'

'I don't know, Ma. Truth is I was fixin' to enlist an' do my bit for the Union.'

He thought the news would make her happy. She'd always believed in the Union. And more than once she'd said that if it ever came to war, the Federal Government was so strong that any conflict would be over in six months.

Instead, her expression changed and she slurred: 'Don't get involved in that business, son. I beg you.'

'But it's my duty, Ma. It's every man's duty to — '

'It's every man's duty to see to his own,' she said with unexpected fire. 'To look after those who need him.'

She was right, to a point. But there was more to it than that and Will knew it. She didn't want him to put himself in anymore danger. To lose him now was something she couldn't possibly withstand.

'Promise me, Will,' she said desperately. 'Promise me you won't get involved.'

'I promise,' he said.

But it was one of the hardest promises he ever had to keep.

★   ★   ★

President Lincoln soon confirmed the existence of an insurrection and called for 75,000 volunteers to stop it. Less than a month later he called for an additional 43,000 recruits, and under any other circumstances Will would have been among the first.

Instead, he stayed home and tended the farm.

As the months dragged on, news came through of various small-scale skirmishes, and then the first real clash of any note — the Battle of Big Bethel, in Virginia. After that, one confrontation followed another as each Union move was met with a Confederate counter-move. Men fought and men died.

And still Will stayed home to keep his promise.

Almost a year passed before he started hearing rumors about the formation of a company of border scouts, personally financed by the Governor of Kansas. By all accounts, these scouts would protect the settlements along the Kansas-Missouri line from the Confederate guerillas who had taken to raiding them. Since the Red Leg Scouts, as the outfit was called, were in no way officially attached to the Union Army, Will felt he could join them without breaking the promise he'd made to his mother.

The Red Legs had established their headquarters at a place called Six Mile House, so-called because it lay six miles from the town of Wyandotte. Led by General Thomas Ewing Jr., and Brigadier General James Blunt, the requisites for membership were absolute loyalty to the Union cause, courage under fire, and the ability to use a firearm to good effect.

One evening Will rode out to Six Mile House with the intention of volunteering. The house was a large, square clapboard affair set in a scraggy field shaded by trees. From a distance he could see that something was going on behind the property — a number of torches had been lit to provide illumination against the dusk, and several horses were picketed in the sloping front yard.

Will dismounted and tied his mount to the picket fence, then stepped onto the front porch. Before he could knock, however, the door opened and a tall, bearded man with a prominent lower jaw appeared. He was wearing Union blue — a double-breasted frock coat with black velvet collar and cuffs, the shoulder boards showing a single star inside a gold-stitched border.

'Help you?' he asked brusquely.

Will took off his hat. 'Are you General Ewing, sir?'

The other man nodded. He was in his early thirties and stood ramrod-straight, as if there were no give in him whatsoever. 'Do I know you, son?'

'No sir. But I'd like to join the Red Legs.'

Ewing's pale face seemed to close up. 'I think you must have the wrong place.'

'No, sir. This *is* Six Mile House, isn't it?'

'I'm sorry, son. I can't help you.'

'But — '

'I am not in the habit of repeating myself *twice*, son,' Ewing warned softly.

Will wanted to argue the point, but

decided against it. 'Then I'm sorry to have troubled you — '

'*Will?*'

Surprised to hear his name mentioned, he looked beyond Ewing, into the house and to his amazement recognized an old friend.

'Wild Bill!'

Hickok came to the door, looking as tall and lean as ever, and still favoring his distinctive Navy Colts tucked in his flamboyant crimson sash. 'My God, it's good to see you!' he said, pumping Will's hand.

General Ewing said: 'You know this boy, Hickok?'

'Know him? Why, him 'n' me is practically brothers! This here's Will Cody, General. His pa was a Free State man, an' God bless him, died for the cause.' He turned his attention back to Will. 'You here to join the Red Legs, you say?'

'That was the idea.'

'Well, you won't find a feller better-suited to the task, General.'

'He's just a boy,' argued Ewing.

'He *might* look like a boy,' Hickok corrected, 'but there's bark on him. I've seen it.'

Ewing hesitated for a few seconds, then made his decision. 'Well . . . if that's the case, you certainly come highly recommended, Mr. Cody. Come on through. We're just about to get down to cases.'

18

Darkness was falling as they went through the house and out into the backyard. Torchlight threw flickering shadows across a gathering of some fifty or sixty men. Ewing excused himself and made his way to an ornate, raised gazebo that served as an impromptu stage.

Will turned to Hickok and said: 'What in hell are *you* doing here?'

'Same thing as you, *compadre*. When the word goes out that my country needs spies and scouts to fight its enemies, you'll never find me shirkin' my duty. Besides, we get to wear these fancy duds.'

Will looked down and saw that Hickok was wearing red yarn leggings, as were all the other men present. They not only identified them as a unit, the leggings would also protect their legs while riding or marching through thick prickly brush. Long dusters and distinctive plumed hats completed their informal uniform.

'You always were a fashion-plate,' Will said, grinning.

'Never mind your funnin',' said Hickok. 'Let's you'n me find a good spot before they get to gabbin'.'

He turned and pushed his way through the throng, Will behind him. As they passed, Will found himself greeted by a number of men he knew, some better than others. Up on the steps of the latticework gazebo, meanwhile, General Ewing was joined by two other men. The first was a dark, square-faced man with a long beard and black, wavy hair. Like Ewing, he was in his middle thirties and he too wore the uniform of a Union officer. The insignia of a brigadier general, however, identified him as James Blunt, a physician in civilian life. The second man was younger, clean-shaven and almost bookish in appearance. He wore a town suit over an open-necked shirt.

Then Ewing cleared his throat and an expectant hush settled over his audience.

'Welcome, gentlemen,' he said. 'As you know, we've been tasked with protecting our border with Missouri, and with good reason. We have no shortage of enemies, but not all of them wear Confederate gray. Some — lowly specimens like William Clarke Quantrill, the James boys, George Todd, the Younger brothers and others — have seen fit to use the excuse of war to conduct their own hit-and-run attacks against our people. They claim to be fighting on behalf of the Confederacy, but my opinion is that they are simply common outlaws, using the chaos and confusion of war to commit crimes for their own end.

He paused and murmurs of agreement came from the audience.

'These guerillas,' Ewing continued, 'are constantly coming in from Missouri to raid, burn and plunder anything and everything of value. And frankly, my friends, the regular Army has enough on its plate as it is right now, without having to send men it cannot spare to watch over our borders. That is where we come in.'

Again Ewing paused and this time Brigadier General Blunt stepped forward. 'So,' he added, 'what can we do to stop these miscreants? Well, in the first place, we can send out spies to learn where and when these guerillas intend to strike next. Armed with that information, we can be there ahead of them and give them a warm welcome when they finally show themselves.

'But such foreknowledge might not always be available to us. Therefore, we propose a simple strategy. If one of the towns or settlements in our care is raided, we will cross the border and raid those Missourians right back! If they burn our buildings, we'll go over there and burn theirs! And if one Kansan dies by their hand, we will ride into Missouri and kill ten for every one we lose! In short, gentlemen, we will fight the dirty war they have chosen to fight, and we'll see how they like it!

'Now,' he said when a spontaneous

round of applause finally died down, 'if there is any man present who does not feel he can fight in such a manner, he is free to leave now, with no hard feelings. But let me warn you — I will expect from those of you who stay, to fight without the slightest vestige of mercy for his enemies.'

There was some uncomfortable shuffling, not least from Will, but no one left.

Ewing again stepped forward. 'The biggest problem we have right now is William Clarke Quantrill,' he said. 'He hit the village of Aubry, in Johnson County, in the most brutal manner. The raiders not only took horses and other property, but also shot innocent civilians in cold blood. Add the likes of Olathe and a few other border towns to the list, and you can see why he's got the people who live up that way scared that they'll be next.

'But Captain George Henry Hoyt, here, late of the Kansas Seventh Volunteer Cavalry, reckons we can catch him by his heels and I believe him! Though new to Kansas, Hoyt is no stranger to the border.'

As Hoyt, the bookish young civilian, stepped forward, there were cheers from the audience and even a smattering of applause. Up close, however, Hoyt didn't look like much. Indeed, he looked downright ill. Only later would Will discover that his poor health had forced him to resign from the Seventh.

'We're going to teach the guerrillas a lesson,' Hoyt assured. 'And sometimes we'll be away from home for weeks at a time to do it! Now, I understand you all have commitments to your families — that's why we're here now, because we want to protect them. But no man should experience financial hardship for having the decency to stand up for his beliefs and to protect that which he holds dear! So General Ewing and Brigadier General Blunt here have agreed to put those men who might otherwise know financial hardship on their payrolls, where they will receive up to seven dollars a day in recompense!'

At a time when an enlisted man was paid thirteen dollars for a whole month, this was a tremendous amount and the onlookers were suitably impressed.

'We will also establish bases of operations here, at Six Mile House, and also in Lawrence and Fort Scott,' Hoyt concluded.

'Gentlemen,' said Ewing, 'though we are not in any way to be considered a part of the Union Army, we are now officially at war, and we have the blessing of our leaders in Washington to give the guerillas hell. So, I ask you — what are we going to give them?'

As one, his audience yelled back: '*Hell!*'

* * *

And they did.

In October, Quantrill and his men raided Shawneetown in Johnson County. En route, they encountered a Union supply train and killed all the civilian

223

drivers and the Union escort. With their blood lust up, they then razed Shawneetown to the ground.

Hoyt and the Red Legs responded by undertaking a grueling three-week expedition in search of Quantrill, which only ended when it was learned that the guerilla leader had gone south to winter in Texas.

By New Year, however, the Red Legs were back in Missouri, burning homes and stealing livestock in retaliation for yet more guerilla attacks on Kansas settlements. Forging as far east as Columbus, they also encouraged untold numbers of slaves to follow them back to Kansas.

In the spring of 1863 the Red Legs, augmented by the 1st Colored Infantry, forged into Lafayette County, burned Chapel Hill and freed an even larger number of slaves.

Knowing his father would have approved, Will took pride in that. But there was no pride to be taken in waging war on a scared civilian population. In that regard, many of his fellow Red Legs were little better than the guerillas they'd been formed to fight.

What made things worse was the reputation the Red Legs acquired along the way — a reputation they didn't always entirely warrant.

One evening at Six Mile House, General Ewing addressed the problem directly.

'It seems that the very people we have sworn to protect are becoming scared of us, gentlemen — even coming to *hate* us . . . and with what they see as good reason. But there is more to this business than meets the eye. I accept fully that there are a few bad apples in our own particular barrel. You know who you are . . . and you might as well know that we will be coming after you in due course, unless you take the opportunity to resign first. But there are also factions out there who are masquerading as Red Legs for their own ends.'

He paused to let his words sink in, then added:

'Now, I'm not saying we're angels. We're not. But we're fighting a *war*, gentlemen, not lining our own pockets. Some of these phony Red Legs have been stealing money, farm equipment, livestock, furniture, crockery, gold and jewelry — in short, anything from which they can make a dishonest dollar. And they're not above killing anyone who tries to stop them. I'm sure you've all heard what happened when our very own Governor Robinson tried to have these imposters run to ground. Yes — they attempted to assassinate him!

'Well, those of us who are *genuine* Red Legs are good at what we do . . . but even *we* can't fight two enemies at once — those dark elements among us who are using and abusing our good name, and those who wage war on behalf of the Confederacy. So for now, we will concentrate our efforts on the Gray Backs. But I will also tell you this, gentlemen. If you should encounter any man who claims to be a Red Leg and *isn't*, if you see any Red Leg who commits an act that is anything less than legitimate in the circumstances at the time . . . you shoot him dead right where he stands. No attempt at arrest. No attempt at court-martial. Just summary execution, plain and simple!'

Subdued, his audience broke up.

Before Will and Hickok could leave, George Hoyt intercepted them. 'The generals would like a word, if you please, gentlemen.'

Will and Hickok exchanged puzzled glances and then followed Hoyt into the house. Ewing and Blunt were seated before the fireplace in the comfortable parlor. They nodded greetings when Will and Hickok stopped before them with hats in hand.

'It's a sorry state of affairs when we no longer know who we can trust,' said Ewing. 'Fortunately, your records are exemplary. We feel confident that we can trust you two entirely.'

'Thanks,' Hickok said cynically.

Ewing let that pass, and said: 'We have an important mission we want you to undertake. It may prove to be dangerous . . . or it may prove to be a complete waste of time. Either way, we've discussed it between us and we feel you two are the only fellows we can entrust with such a duty. So — are you in or out, gentlemen?'

'I'm in,' Will said without hesitation.

Hickok shook his head. 'You'll have to excuse my friend, here. He's young an' headstrong. I think what he really meant to say is that we'd both prefer to hear what this mission *is* first.'

'Fair enough,' said Ewing. 'As I said in my address earlier, the very people we have sworn to protect are now viewing us with fear and suspicion. They no longer feel we can guarantee their safety, not from the guerillas, the Confederates themselves, or the outlaws who have assumed our identity for their own ends. Neither does it help that we have a base in Lawrence, gentlemen. There, in particular, the locals fear reprisals from the likes of Quantrill's Raiders, while Quantrill himself has been most vocal in his hatred of the Red Legs.

'George Collamore, the mayor of Lawrence, is convinced that Quantrill intends to raid the town. The opinion of the military is that such a raid is unlikely for several reasons. They argue that Quantrill cannot possibly penetrate the military line on the border without detection. They feel sure, too, that he cannot cross thirty-five miles of enemy territory to reach his objective without someone, somewhere, raising the alarm.

'I do not disagree with them, gentlemen. But still the rumors of a raid persist. And we know Quantrill of old. He has audacity, and a tendency to do what his enemies least expect.'

'So what's our job, General?' asked Hickok.

'There's something else we know about Quantrill,' said Blunt. 'He rarely does anything on the spur of the moment. He thinks, he plans, he reconnoiters, and only when he's sure he will be successful in any given endeavor, does he make his move.

'If he does indeed plan to raid Lawrence, he will scout the town thoroughly first. So we want you two to go up there and see if you can find any evidence to suggest that he has done or is about to do that very thing.

'If he *is* planning something, and we can be there ahead of him and protect those citizens, then it will go a long way toward restoring their confidence in our integrity as fighting men.' He paused to let that sink in and then said: 'Well — are you game?'

'Yes, sir,' Will said, almost before Blunt had finished speaking.

Hickok was a little more guarded. 'We'll take a look around,' he said.

Ewing stood up. 'Thank you, gentlemen. As I say, it may be a complete waste of time or it may prove to be a messy business indeed. You will stay at the Johnson House Hotel as usual.'

The Johnson House doubled as the Red Legs' short-term headquarters whenever they visited Lawrence.

'We'll leave first thing in the mornin',' said Hickok, saluting.

As they left the room, Will glanced at the calendar on the wall.

It was August 19, 1863.

19

Lawrence was situated along the banks of the Kansas and Wakarusa Rivers, a little less than forty miles west of the Missouri border. Founded close to a decade earlier on what had once been Shawnee land, it was a well-known Free State stronghold, and as such no stranger to violence. Still, everything looked peaceful enough when Will and Hickok rode in the following noon and headed directly for the Johnson House.

Although the town had a population of around two thousand, there was plenty of space between dwellings, and the grid system upon which Lawrence had been built showed that it was ready and able to expand as its population grew.

'You're quiet today, Will,' Hickok noted as they stabled their horses in the barn at the far end of the hotel's long backyard.

'Am I?'

'You know damn'-well you are. What's on your mind?'

Will hesitated before saying: 'The Red Legs.'

Hickok looked at him. 'What about 'em?'

'I'm not sure I want to be one anymore.'

'I know *that* feelin',' Hickok replied. 'You fight because you think it's the right thing to do, and it *is*, when you're fightin' the enemy. But sometimes it's hard to think of all those ordinary folks across the line there as the enemy.'

'Well, I've turned a blind eye about as long as I can,' said Will, glad to finally get it off his chest. 'I've tried to make allowances . . . you know, that sometimes men do things in the heat of battle that they wouldn't do any other time or place. But some of the fellas we ride with . . . 'pears to me they enjoy killin' a mite too much.'

'Well, you volunteered for it, Will. You can as easily up an' quit.'

'I intend to. My ma ain't gettin' any better, Bill. As much as anythin', I reckon I should spend some time with her while I still can.'

'You do that,' said Hickok. 'Hell, I might even join you, if your sister's the cook you say she is! Tell you what. We'll see what we can find out here — if anythin' — an' after we report back to Ewing tomorrow, you can kick the Red Leg dust off your heels.'

Their first stop was the office of Mayor Collamore. A short, balding man with lively eyes and an affable manner, he eyed them suspiciously at first and then admitted confidentially: 'I've seen no evidence of anyone coming in to get the lay of the land, so to speak. But I hear that Quantrill has been busy, gathering as many outlaw gangs together as he can, so he's clearly planning *something*.'

'Is this fact or hearsay, mayor?' asked Hickok.

'Well, I'd have to say hearsay, inasmuch as I don't have anything to back it up. But you know what they say — you can't have smoke without fire.'

Their next stop was the United Brethren church of Reverend Samuel Snyder. In addition to being the local minister, Snyder also served as a lieutenant in the 2nd Colored Regiment, so he was used to keeping his eyes open and watching for strangers passing through and asking questions.

A lean, elderly man with a liver-spotted pate surrounded by a wispy crown of white hair, he could only say: 'I've been watching, boys, believe me. But if Quantrill's sent out any scouts, I sure haven't seen them.'

The office of the *Kansas State Journal* was next on their list, but again no one had anything suspicious to report. As the editor pointed out: 'The only folks who've been asking around about anything, are *you* two.'

Finally, as the afternoon wound down, they rode up to Hogback Ridge, a hill that overlooked the town, and searched for any signs that might suggest that someone had been keeping the town under observation recently. Once again they came up empty.

'What does that leave?' Will asked over supper that evening.

Hickok shrugged. 'The only thing I can think of is to ride into Missouri and see what we can pick up there.'

Will had ordered roast mutton and vegetables. Now he stopped chewing and looked at his companion. 'An' you think they'd be likely to *tell* us?'

'Only one way to find out, *compadre*.'

They bedded down early that night, but Will found sleep elusive. Now that he'd made his decision to leave the Red Legs he felt better, but his shame at having taken part in so much senseless violence left him feeling somehow unclean.

The August night was warm. Around two in the morning he got up, went to the window and looked down into Main Street. Nothing stirred.

He was just about to go back to bed

when he heard the sound of hoof beats in the distance, approaching at a walk. Curious, he stayed at the window, peering through the lace, until three men rode past the hotel, looking neither left nor right.

He watched them until they were out of sight, wondering who they were and what they were doing riding into town at such an ungodly hour. Unable to come up with an answer, and as certain as he could be that their intentions were peaceable, he went back to bed.

He wasn't aware that he'd dozed off until he heard the gunfire.

★ ★ ★

Leaping out of bed, he grabbed for the Dragoon, hanging in its holster over the bedpost. On the other side of the room, ghostly in his white combinations, Wild Bill was doing likewise. The tin clock on the dresser told them it was five in the morning.

'What — ?'

Will poked his head through the window. 'There's a bunch of men outside the church,' he hissed. And then: 'No!'

'What?'

'Looks like they dragged Snyder out into the street an' shot him dead!'

A second ticked into history as they looked at each other. *Snyder.* No one could possibly want to kill a preacher, surely? But a preacher who doubled as a lieutenant in a Union regiment . . . ?

Will said what they were both thinking.

'*Quantrill!*'

As if to confirm it, the town suddenly exploded with the wild, ululating cry of rebels, and a long line of horsemen came galloping along Main, firing their guns in every direction.

Will and Hickok threw themselves to the floor as the window shattered.

'Well, Ewing's got his answer,' Wild Bill said as they quickly dressed. 'An' there's not a damn thing we can do about it!'

Outside, all hell was breaking loose, particularly to the west of town. Men were yelling, women were screaming, babies were crying — and over it all came the steady, remorseless crackle of gunfire and smashing glass. There was also some kind of separate skirmish going on down along the bank of the river, where a detachment of the Kansas 14th had been encamped. It sounded as if the Kansans were getting the worst of it.

'How do we play this?' asked Will.

'How do you think? We get out of here, *pronto!*'

'You do that,' said Will. 'I'll stand an' fight.'

'You won't be standin' for long,' Hickok assured him.

Will wanted to argue the point, but knew Hickok was right. Much as he hated to run, it was all they could do in the circumstances. Quantrill considered every Red Leg a sworn enemy. If he caught them, and realized they were Red Legs, then all they could expect was a bullet — maybe a bunch of them.

Hickok chanced a look out the splintered window. The town was heaving now, as guerillas cantered back and forth, hurling burning torches through the windows of buildings and shooting at anyone who to dared to show themselves on the streets.

'Jesus wept!' he spat. 'There's hundreds of 'em! Come on — we've got to get to the stable, grab our horses an' ride.'

As Hickok opened the door, Will spotted a silhouette out in the hallway. He had the Dragoon cocked and ready for a chest shot when the man said: 'Don't fire! It's me — Alexander Banks!'

Banks, provost marshal of the state, was also staying at the hotel. A short, blue-eyed man with a scraggly goatee beard, he said: 'Where do you think you're goin'?'

'We're gettin' out while we still can,' said Hickok.

'*Runnin'*, in other words.'

'Me, I call it self-preservation.'

'What's *your* plan, captain?' asked Will.

'Surrender,' Banks said reluctantly.

'Surrender?' Hickok repeated in disbelief. 'Hell, that's *Quantrill* down there! I'd sooner trust a gut-shot grizzly!'

'Well, that's what we're goin' to do!'

'Your funeral,' said Hickok. 'Come on, Will.'

They pushed past him and hurried downstairs. Fires were breaking out in the buildings across the street, the flames filling the lobby with shifting shadows. Out front a guerilla caught hold of a woman in a nightdress and dragged her off into an alleyway.

'I can't go,' said Will abruptly.

'You can't *stay*.'

'I mean, I got to do what I can to fight back.'

Hickok felt the same way, but was wise enough to know that fighting back right then would be as good as committing suicide. 'If it's a fight you want,' he rasped, 'you'll have one just tryin' to get as far as the stable.'

He went around the counter and into a small back office. Will hesitated and then started toward the locked front doors. As he approached them, a large body of riders thundered up and spread out before the hotel. Immediately he drew back and dropped to a crouch.

After the newcomers drew rein, an unsettling quiet seemed to descend over that section of the town.

'*Will!*' hissed Hickok.

Will scurried back across the lobby and joined Hickok into the back office. Wild Bill carefully drew back the bolts and turned the key to unlock the door.

'*Quantrill!*'

They froze, but realized almost immediately that it was Banks, calling down to the guerillas from the window of his room.

'William Clarke Quantrill, are you out there?' he shouted. 'We surrender, provided you guarantee the safety of every person here!'

The response was just what Wild Bill had expected. A sudden explosion of gunfire riddled the front of the hotel, shattering windows, splintering frames and bullets whining off brickwork.

'That damn fool!' Hickok hissed. Then he opened the back door and ran out into the muggy pre-dawn with Will at his heels.

Almost at once Hickok threw himself sideways, into the cover of some brush. Will followed suit, for the stable on the far side of the backyard was already being ransacked by more of Quantrill's raiders.

As the men chased the stabled horses out and off to the east, Will whispered: 'Now what?'

By way of answer, Hickok ran to the corner of the building and disappeared down a narrow alleyway that fed through to Main. Will followed him, close behind.

The shooting out front had now died down. When Will and Hickok came to a pile of empty crates and barrels that had been stacked just short of the alley mouth, they didn't take any chances but took cover. Chancing a look through gaps in the garbage, they saw that Captain Banks and the hotel's other lodgers were being escorted across Winthrop Street by several raiders. Just before they reached the far boardwalk, a guerilla rode out of nowhere and brought his horse to a sliding halt beside them.

'You, there!' he called, jabbing his gun at one man in particular. 'Step out here!'

The object of his attention was a scared, barefoot youngster who'd only had time to pull a pair of pants up over his red combinations. He looked at Banks for guidance, and after a moment Banks nodded.

As soon as the youngster stepped away from the rest of the prisoners, the rider shot at him twice. Amazingly, both bullets missed. Swearing, the raider took aim again and prepared to fire a third shot, but a new voice bellowed a single word.

'*No!*'

A second rider galloped onto the scene astride a spirited blue roan. 'Save your bullets for those who can shoot back!' he snapped, struggling to hold the horse in check. He was tall, dark and squint-eyed, with a cadaverous face, much of it hidden beneath a heavy mustache and a long, black beard. His equally black, disheveled hair stuck out from beneath a flat-topped slouch hat worn at a jaunty angle.

Hickok breathed: 'That's him.'

'Him, who?' Will asked.

'That's *Quantrill*.'

20

Will brought his Dragoon Colt up. 'Much as I hate to shoot any man from hidin',' he grated, 'I might be able to stop all *this* if I stop *him*.'

Hickok quickly knocked the long barrel down. 'Show sense, damn you!

'I — '

'Look at those men out there! They're fired enough up as it is! Kill Quantrill and you'll only make things worse.'

'They don't look like they could *get* much worse.'

'Best you don't try an' find out.'

In the street now Quantrill was addressing the men who had been guarding Banks and his companions. 'Take 'em up to the City Hotel,' he said, gesturing toward the river. 'I stayed there once, and was well-treated. You prisoners! You'll be unharmed if you do as we say! Rest of you fellas . . . ' and here he gestured to the Johnson House, ' . . . burn this place to the ground!'

As he rode off, Will muttered: 'Maybe we should've surrendered after all.'

'I ain't so sure. I still got a bad feeling about this.'

As it turned out, Hickok was right to have doubts. Another band of guerillas had just finished storming the Eldridge Hotel, next door, and ordered the inhabitants to give themselves up. A few moments later a handful of townsfolk stepped out onto the boardwalk with their hands held high. The guerillas marched them about two hundred feet farther along the street, then shot them all dead, one after another.

Will gripped the Dragoon even tighter. 'I don't understand! Why — '

'Because this is a lottery,' Hickok said disgustedly. 'It all depends on who you run into an' how he feels at the time! One of these fellas will take you prisoner, the next one'll gun you down

just for the pleasure of seein' you fall.'
A new thought struck him, and he
slapped Will on the arm. 'Remember
the ravine that runs along the edge of
town? Might be the safest place to be
about now.'

Cautiously, they ventured out onto
the street. Around them, the town
resembled hell on fire. Half-dressed
townsmen lay dead or wounded in the
street, as did women and children. A
few brave souls had ventured out to
tend the injured, and every so often a
blast of dynamite would shake the
ground, as Quantrill's men hit the
banks and blew their safes.

On the far side of Main, two guerillas
were smashing open the door of a
general store with the intention of
looting it. When one of them caught
sight of Will and Hickok, he bawled a
warning to his companion. Even as they
reached for their revolvers, Wild Bill
shot them both and Will watched them
drop with grim relish.

Sticking to whatever cover they could

find, they managed to make another fifty yards. Then, as they were crossing an alleyway, Will heard something that stopped him — a baby crying.

He turned toward the sound, saw a woman in a torn nightdress trying to crouch in the shadows with the baby in her arms, and two more children, wide-eyed and terrified, clinging to her.

'P-Please . . . ' she begged. 'P-please don't kill my children . . . '

'It's all right,' said Will. 'We're not with Quantrill.'

'We're gettin' out of here,' added Hickok, going to her and taking the baby. 'An' I think we better take you with us.'

The woman looked from one of them to the other. Shocked by the events of the dawn, she didn't seem to fully understand Wild Bill had said. When she turned her large, violet eyes back to Will, he nodded and extended one hand. 'Come on, ma'am. Best we get movin'.'

Will led the way, the woman and the two older children shuffling along behind him, and Wild Bill fetching up the rear, rocking the baby in one arm as he tried to keep a watch on everything at once. Guerillas rode back and forth, shooting at those few townspeople who were trying to organize resistance, and most of the buildings were now burning.

Without warning, two guerillas trotted their mounts out of an alley ten feet ahead of them. One of them glanced their way and just for a second, in the slowly building light, his eyes met those of Will. Then the guerilla hooked at his Remington and Will shot him in the cheek. The man spilled backward, spoiling the aim of his equally surprised companion.

As the woman screamed in fear Will shot the second man. The bullet caught the guerilla in the throat and both of them fell lifelessly to the hardpan.

The outskirts of town now lay directly ahead, and he could see that they weren't the only ones heading for the narrow, wooded ravine and possible escape. A number of townsfolk were racing toward it. Several guerillas had dismounted and were trying to shoot at them as they went, but none of them wanted to chase them into the ravine itself, which offered some cover from which the locals might fight back.

Near at hand, a gunshot tore through all the chaos. Will turned in time to see Wild Bill's bullet hit a guerilla who had shown himself on a balcony of a saloon across the street. The man grabbed at his bloody chest and then fell forward over the balustrade to land with a sickening thud.

Will and Hickok started picking up the pace, heading for the relative safety of the brush and trees, where the guerillas couldn't see them well enough to pick them off. The ground sloped downward, a carpet of grass and weeds replaced dirt and dust, and before they knew it they were part of an exodus of townsfolk, some weeping, others leaning against trees to get their breath, yet more stumbling along like sleepwalkers, all of them shocked to the core by what had happened and what they'd endured.

An elderly man with his white hair awry saw them coming and took the baby from Wild Bill's arms. Will looked at the woman and her children, and she looked back at him with nothing in her face except sorrow.

'My husband was back there,' she managed at last. 'They *killed* him.'

It was a stupid thing to say, but he said it anyway. 'I'm sorry, ma'am.'

Then Wild Bill pushed him forward and they continued jogging along the ravine, heading west.

The morning continued to lighten slowly. After a time the ravine opened out onto a patchwork of fields. Behind them, Lawrence burned steadily, belching black smoke toward the pink sky of a new day.

Indicating a cornfield to their left, Hickok said: 'Come on, we'll lose ourselves in there. Once Quantrill's gone, we'll sneak back and try to find a couple horses.'

Swatting cornstalks aside, Hickok plunged into the field. Will hesitated on the edge, as haunted by the smells of dirt and honey and flower-scent as he had been since he was nine years old.

Hickok looked back at him. 'What's wrong?'

Will made no reply.

'Will?'

'Nothin',' he said at length. And then, as if with all the weariness in the world: 'Let's get out of here.'

21

Despite a strong desire to get revenge on Quantrill, Will quit the Red Leg Scouts just as he'd said he would and soon found work as a guide with the 9th Kansas Cavalry. For the rest of that year, while the Civil War continued to rage, he and the 9th fought the Kiowas and Comanches who were raising hell along the Santa Fe Trail.

By the end of the year the Indians had been pacified, and Will wrote home to say he would be spending Christmas with his family.

The night he got back, a strong, cold wind was blowing through the corn-field, making the stalks rustle and shake. He saw to his horse, then hurried toward the house, the plainsman in him sensing a coming ice storm.

Although it was late, lamplight filled the downstairs windows. But when he came through the door and unbuttoned his greatcoat, he found only Julia waiting for him on the sofa. Around them, the rest of the house was quiet but for the occasional creak of timbers when the wind blew especially strong.

He took one look at his sister's face and saw at once that the news was not good.

'Ma — ' he began.

'Thank God you're back,' Julia said tearfully. 'She's not long for this world now, Will.'

He took a moment to digest that, then said: 'Is she awake?'

'I don't think so.'

'I'll go up and look in on her anyway, sis.' He went upstairs and opened the door to his mother's bedroom. His mother was just a still, indistinct shape in the bed. Only her uneasy breathing disturbed the otherwise heavy hiss of silence, and he was just about to turn away when she said out of the darkness: 'Will? Is that you?'

He entered and closed the door softly

behind him. 'Yes, Ma.'

He sat on the edge of her bed. There was no light in the room save moonlight, in which she looked hollow and lifeless.

'How you feelin', Ma?'

'Tired, Will,' she said. 'Awful tired.' She stirred a little. 'I was dreaming . . . remembering when I was your age. Hadn't met your pa then . . . was traveling by steamboat along the Ohio. Cousin Grace was with me.' She paused, as a new thought occurred to her. 'Never did meet Cousin Grace, did you, Will?'

'No, Ma.'

'Two of us went ashore at Louisville, and just for fun had our . . . fortunes told . . . Know what she told me, Will? Said I was going to meet a man on the trip . . . that I'd have three sons, one of whom I must give to the world. Said he'd be famous . . . that everyone would praise him.' With great effort, she brought one thin hand out from over the covers and put it over his.

'Fortune-teller meant *you*, Will. Second son, she said. Name'll be in the history books ... be remembered forever ... just like kings and queens and presidents ...'

Her voice tailed off and her eyes — so liquid in the moonlight — closed. For an awful moment he thought that she was dead. But then the eyes opened again, and she smiled. 'Going to make me and your pa so proud, Will,' she murmured. 'So proud.'

He couldn't picture himself like she'd described and decided that her mind was wandering. But anxious to please her, he said: 'Well, that's all that matters to me, Ma. That you and pa think — '

He stopped, realizing that he could no longer hear her tortuous breathing.

'Ma?' he asked, as if he might be mistaken.

There was no response.

'Ma . . . ?'

Nothing.

He lifted her cold lifeless hand to his

mouth and kissed it.

Then he wept.

* * *

With his mother gone, he was now free to enlist in the army. And as soon as the New Year got underway, he did just that. Within months, Will's outfit, the 7th Kansas Volunteers, traveled to Memphis, Tennessee, by steamboat, where it was absorbed into the command of General A. J. Smith, who was then organizing an army to fight the Confederate General Bedford Forrest.

But for Will, the greatest battle of his life was still to come.

Part Six — Buffalo Hunter

22

The war ended when General Robert E. Lee surrendered to Lieutenant General Ulysses S. Grant at Appomattox Courthouse, Virginia, on April 9, 1865. Once discharged from his unit, Will returned to his home state and found work driving herds of army horses between Fort Leavenworth, Kansas, and Fort Kearny, Nebraska. In his spare time he also worked as a stagecoach driver. But though work kept him busy, he felt rootless now that his mother was gone. There seemed no purpose to his life and in his heart he missed the great open plains more and more.

One afternoon, when he was pondering his uncertain future over a warm beer in the Fort Leavenworth sutler's store, an elderly, near-sighted man with a downy gray beard cast his shadow across the table and asked Will if he might take a seat.

Will glanced at the newcomer. He was short and stringy, a little back-bent, and dressed in a soiled black Prince Albert over a faded red undershirt. He wore thick spectacles, but still had to squint his hazel eyes half-shut in order to see Will clearly.

'It's a free country,' Will replied.

'Aye, it is, *now*,' said the other man amiably, his accent unmistakably Scottish. He settled himself opposite Will and briefly studied the glass of cloudy whisky he'd just purchased. Then, looking up again, he said: 'You'd be Will Cody, I'm thinking.'

Will eyed him a little closer. 'Do I know you, mister?'

'Nae, laddie. But you're *goin'* to.' He raised his glass. 'I'm Scotty McNichols, by the way. Here's to health an' prosperity for the both of us.'

'I'll drink to that,' said Will.

'Don't exactly taste o' the heather,' Scotty decided after swilling the whiskey around his few remaining teeth, 'but it'll wash the burrs from a man's throat, I suppose.' 'How come you know my name?' asked Will.

'Och, ye cannae be that modest, laddie! You're famous in these parts, so they tell me! Killed your fust man when you was little more than a bairn in arms, drove cattle when you was ten, rode the longest distance over the most dangerous section of the route when you worked for the Pony Express — three hundred and twenty two miles in less than twenty-four hours, if I'm nae mistaken.'

'The horses, they did all the work.'

'Och, pish-posh! There were twenty-one horses, laddie, but only one of you!'

'Where'd you hear all this nonsense, anyway?'

'Let's just say I keep my ear to the ground. An' when I hear about a lad like yoursen, not yet twenty-one years old, a lad who can pretty much hang the moon if he takes a notion to do so, and can shoot better than fair — '

Will cut him off. 'If you're a

salesman, mister, I'm not buyin'.'

'I'm nae about to charge ye for the privilege of gettin' rich, William. That's an opportunity I'm givin' you free, *gratis* an' for nothin'.'

'What's the catch?'

'There's no catch, laddie! All I'm suggestin' is a simple partnership an' a straight fifty-fifty cut on everythin' we earn. And we *will* earn, William. We'll earn more money than you can imagine.'

'I'm not in the business of robbin' banks, Mr. McNichols.'

'Call me Scotty, laddie, everyone does. As for robbin' banks . . . och, that's hard work compared to what *we'll* be doin'.'

Although Will wasn't entirely convinced by Scotty's fine talk, he couldn't help but like the man and become just a tad curious. 'All right — let's hear it.'

Scotty threw a glance out the window at the plains beyond the fort. 'Our destiny's out there, laddie. That's where we find the commodity that's going tae make us rich.'

'Say it plain.'

'Buffalo, William,' said the Scotsman. 'Millions an' millions of the beasties . . . an' each one good as gold in our pockets, if we play this thing right.'

'What thing?'

'You shoot 'em an' I'll skin 'em, laddie. And if things go the way I expect, we'll earn ourselves a fortune.'

'Are you crazy? I'm not shootin' buffalo for a livin'.'

'Why not?'

'It's too much like shootin' quail in a bucket. There's no sport in it.'

'It's not supposed to *be* a sport, William. It's a business . . . an' if you can shoot as good as everyone says, it cannae help but be a profitable one. For both of us.'

'Maybe so. But I ain't interested.'

'Listen to me, laddie. I told you I keep my ear to the ground. I do. That's how come I know the Union Pacific's about to start runnin' tracks from Lawrence to Junction City and beyond.'

'Everyone knows that.'

'Aye. But when they set to work, they'll need to feed their workers. I also happen to know that they're prepared to pay top dollar for fresh meat. But that, William, is only the half of it.'

'Go on.'

'The meat we sell feeds the railway workers, right? The tongues we sell separately, because they're becomin' a delicacy back East, an' they'll fetch a better price. We sell their bones to the folks who crush 'em down to make fertilizer, an' their hides, laddie, by God, the market for their hides is just openin' up an' Leavenworth is goin' to be one of the biggest and the busiest! We cannae lose, William. Even the army cannae encourage men like us enough.'

Will scowled. 'What's the army got to do with it?'

'Well, let's just say they approve of us . . . thinnin' the herd, so to speak. We work hard, we could earn maybe six or seven hundred dollars a month . . . an' that disnae include what we'll make off the hides.'

The figure stunned Will. 'Six or seven *hundred . . . ?*'

'Aye. Maybe more. Been a butcher all my life, William, an' I ain't never seen a bigger meat market than the one on hoof out there.'

Though tempted, Will still hesitated.

Scotty said: 'I'm offerin' you the chance to get rich, boy. Hell, what else you got to do right now?'

'Nothin'.'

'Well, *nothin's* a mighty poor partner, 'specially when there's a fortune just a-waitin' to be had.' He could see that he was slowly winning Will over, and added persuasively: 'Look, if it's the buffalo that's troublin' you . . . och, the little amount we kill, compared to millions that are out there, it'll be no more'n like steppin' on a few ants. Besides, once we've made some money, if you still don't like it, you quit an' I'll find me another hunter. Good enough?'

Will wasn't exactly happy about it. It seemed like a desperate, unpleasant way to make a living. But he *could* use the money, if only to help the brother and sisters he still felt that he had abandoned. And buffalo hunting would take him back to his beloved plains.

Hesitantly, he nodded, and accepted the Scotsman's gnarled hand when it was offered.

'Partners it is, then,' said Scotty.

And partners it was.

23

Having thrown in with Scotty, Will decided he had better do the job properly. Thanks to Oscar Purebright, he'd seen first-hand just how hard it could be to kill a buffalo. If he was going to do it at all, he wanted to make sure that every kill was clean, and that the animal itself knew little if anything about it.

While Scotty spent such money as he had on supplies, and readied his disreputable old red-wheeled, green-boxed Shüttler wagon for travel, Will bought a .50-caliber Springfield rifle. It was, the storekeeper assured him, the best gun ever made for killing buffalo.

'Them that's got one call it a 'needle' gun,' he said.

Will looked up from his examination of the weapon. 'Why?'

'On account of the firin' pin.' The

storekeeper indicated the part in question — and Will had to confess, it did indeed resemble a needle. 'They claim it never misfires.'

'All right,' said Will. 'I'll take it.'

Later, when he met up with Scotty, the little butcher nodded approvingly at Will's purchase. 'Looks to me like we're in business,' he grinned. 'Put your gun in the back of yon wagon, laddie, and we'll think about where we start.'

Will did as he was told. It was the first time he'd looked inside Scotty's wagon, and its contents — skinning blades, chains, sledgehammers and grindstones — only fueled his unease.

'Now,' said the Scotsman, 'let's go find us a buffalo herd.'

* * *

There was one thing you could say for Scotty McNichols — he knew how to find buffalo. Whenever Will asked him how he did it, the little Scotsman would only shrug, as if it were no big thing.

The truth was, he didn't want anyone else to know. But in truth it was a combination of things, the most important of which were how well-grazed the country was and how close it was to water.

Within a week of their association, they located a small herd and Will undertook his first hunt. The buffalo were scattered across a broad tall-grass plain fringed by scrub and cottonwoods.

With the wagon parked well back from the herd, Will gathered his gear — the .50-caliber Springfield, an iron fork upon which he would rest and steady the weight of the weapon and a bag of greased metallic cartridges.

Finding good cover upwind of the herd in a run of saltbush, he settled down, trying to ignore his continued misgivings about the killing to come. It was one thing to kill in order to put meat on the table. But to kill for money, even to kill such seemingly dumb beasts like the buffalo now spread out before him . . . it still didn't set right with him. But he could hardly back out now. He'd given his word.

He shoved the iron fork into the ground and then stretched out on his belly. Settling the Springfield's long, slender barrel in its supportive V, he calculated firing angles that would allow for windage and elevation. When he was satisfied, he loaded the Springfield.

After that he could delay the moment no longer.

His first target was a big, elderly bull that was chewing the cud on the far fringe of the herd. Will had identified him as the leader, the one who would be most likely to raise the alarm when the shooting began.

He shot the bull just where the animal's ribcage ended. The gun roared and punched against his shoulder. The bull collapsed, shot through the lungs.

Incredibly, the animals surrounding the bull didn't even look at him. And that was the hell of it. These massively powerful animals were so docile in their way, and still so relatively unused to the ways of the white man, that they showed no signs of panic. They simply didn't understand what had just happened or what was *still* to happen.

Time and again the morning peace was shattered by the steady, rhythmic boom of the Springfield. After each blast, a buffalo dropped heavily to the grass. Most were killed outright. Will regretted every death that took longer. The slaughter — and he could think of no other word for it — went on and on.

When he'd had his fill and didn't think he could possibly take another life, he climbed back to his feet and saw that he had shot the twelve buffalo their contract with the U.P. called for. If he continued — even if he'd had the *inclination* to continue — he was bound to miss a direct kill soon or later, and the cries of the wounded buffalo would cause the rest of the herd to panic and flee.

Slick with sweat, Will returned to the

wagon, where Scotty had set a fire and boiled coffee. It was when the Scotsman handed him a mug that Will realized his hand was no longer entirely steady.

'You'll get used to it,' Scotty said, climbing to the wagon seat.

'I doubt that,' Will replied.

Scotty eyed him curiously. 'You wait 'til you're holdin' more money than ye know what to do with.'

Will doubted that any amount of money would wash away the dirty feeling this morning's work had left him.

He flopped down beside the fire and poured himself more coffee. He could manage that, but his belly was too unsettled to manage food. That would have to wait.

Scotty, meanwhile, drove his wagon down among the dead. At last the remaining buffalos stirred a little and started to drift away. Using a knife to finish off any beast in which the faintest spark of life still flickered, he started skinning.

From a distance, Will watched as the Scotsman made his first cut from the lower jaw, down the neck and straight along the belly until he reached a spot just below the tail. Then he scored the inside of each leg, and finally began the business of peeling the hide back with a specially curved knife. At last, with the carcass rolled over and the hide all but removed, he tied a line around the skin still attached to the buffalo's hump and used one of the team-horses to tear it free.

Watching with morbid fascination, Will tossed the remainder of the coffee aside and thought: *What have I done?*

Scotty was wrong. He *was* wrong. There was no way he would ever get used to this.

But the hell of it was — Scotty was right.

He *did* get used to it.

* * *

Over the next eighteen months the killing continued. And as Will's tally mounted, folks began calling him

'Buffalo Bill'. When he got tired of the nagging guilt that assailed him after every hunt, he hit the bottle until, inside, he became someone else.

That Buffalo Bill enjoyed the celebrity that came with his achievement — if the killing of more than four thousand buffalo could be called such — and when he was drunk he played up to the expectations of his admirers. He dressed less like a plainsman and more like a greenhorn. He grew a flowing mustache and a trimmed goatee. And whenever the doubts came creeping back in, as they always did, sooner or later, he did what Scotty had told him to do, and thought about the money.

The money was nothing less than astounding and easily matched every assurance Scotty had given him. But try as he might, Will could only discount the truth of his dirty business for so long.

With the war over, the country was opening up for settlement. There was just one problem — the Indians. When Washington decided that the Indians had to be moved off their ancestral lands to make way for the white man, General Philip Sheridan was sent to beat them into submission. But with an army that was severely under strength, and an enemy that had its own unique method of combat, Sheridan quickly realized he had to find a way to subdue them more effectively.

He found it in the buffalo.

The Indians — the Blackfeet, the Gros Ventre, Assiniboin, Crow, Cheyenne, Shoshoni, Arapaho, Sioux, Comanche and others — relied on the buffalo for practically everything. The buffalo supplied them with food and clothing, bedding and bowstrings, arrow points, bow parts, fuel and glue. Without the buffalo there were no tools, no weapons and no medicine. There was no thread with which the squaws could sew, no rope with which the braves could catch and corral horses.

If you deprived the Indian of the

buffalo, you deprived him of his means to survive.

And that was what Scotty had meant, the day they'd first met. *Even the army can't encourage men like us enough,* he'd said. And when Will had called him on it: *Well, let's just say they approve of us . . . thinnin' the herd, so to speak.*

But hunting alone couldn't bring about the extinction of the buffalo, or the Indians fast enough for the politicians. So the hunting of buffalo was promoted as a sport as well as a business. The Union Pacific started running special trains to take men out to the plains, where they could shoot the buffalo for no other reason than to sell its hide, deprive the Indians of the means he needed to exist, or simply for the thrill of the kill.

Will had seen it once. Hundreds of men, scrambling onto the roofs of trains, or pointing their railroad-supplied weapons from windows and platforms, so they could take aim, fire and kill, and then congratulate each other and boast about what a fine job they were doing on behalf of the government.

But if that was fighting, then it was the dirtiest fighting of all, because it wasn't war waged on warriors, it was war waged on the elderly, the infirm, the women, the babies, the defenseless. Not only that — there was a very real danger that the buffalo itself *would* be hunted to extinction.

One night, Will dreamed about his first meeting with Jim Bridger and Kit Carson. Wild Bill had said: *I promise you, Will — the nearest thing your kids'll ever get to the land as it is right now is you tellin' 'em how it was.*

And Carson had agreed. *As you say. But you're one of the lucky ones, William — born while she still lasts. Now all you got to do is make the most of it.*

Will awoke with a start and sat up breathing hard. Reaching into his bedroll, he took out his now-constant companion, a bottle of whiskey. He thought about the buffalo, the Indians, the direction his life had taken, and then he took a drink . . . and kept drinking until he passed out and there were no more dreams.

24

There was no point in dressing it up, so he just came right out with it.

'I'm through, Scotty.'

He had come to see Scotty at Scotty's hotel room in Fort Hays. The little Scotsman, in shirtsleeves and with his downy gray hair awry, peered up at him. 'What? What d'ye mean, finished?'

'With this,' Will replied, making a wide, meaningless gesture with one hand. He was still a little drunk, and that scared him, because he was no longer sure that he could get through the day sober. 'The huntin'. The killin'. I've had it.'

'Now listen here, William ... you can't just up an' quit! We have a contract to fulfill, mouths to feed! How do you suppose the U.P.'s goin' to take it if we break that contract?'

'We don't *have* a contract no more,

Scotty! In case you've forgotten, construction's been abandoned for the time bein', 'til Sheridan gets a handle on the Indian trouble *he* created.'

'Aye, but that willnae take long, laddie. Sheridan's here himself now, in Fort Hays! He's handlin' the Indians personal-like!'

'I have a feelin' the Indians will handle *him*.'

Scotty shook his head impatiently. 'Be that as it may, what about you? You're Buffalo Bill Cody, for God's sake! You're a celebrity! You're a wealthy man, laddie, and you owe it all to the buffalo!'

'If that's supposed to make me feel any better, it don't.'

'Well, what's the problem? What's gotten into ye all of a sudden?'

Will drew a breath. 'There's nothin' sudden about it. It's been comin' on for months now, but I've been fightin' it. Fightin' it any way I can.' He swallowed and his voice choked slightly as he finished: 'I can't fight it no more.'

Scotty took him by one arm, and spoke in a more conciliatory tone. 'Look, laddie, I can see you're a little the worse for wear. Go on home and sleep it off. You'll feel differently tomorrow.'

'No, I won't. It's finished, Scotty. There's got to be a better way to make money. Maybe I'll go back to scoutin'.'

Scotty looked at him, then said gently: 'Your mind's *really* made up, son?'

Will nodded.

'Well . . . I'll miss you.'

He offered his hand and they shook.

'I only hope you dinnae regret turnin' your back on all this.'

Will raised an eyebrow. 'On killin'? On helpin' to wipe out the buffalo and the Indian both? You don't have to fret on that score.'

He turned, walked unsteadily to the door and let himself out.

★　★　★

He was crossing the lobby and heading for the street when a voice stopped him.

'Mr. Cody?'

He turned, in no mood to talk to anyone, but the speaker's appearance came as a surprise. He was a short, overweight man in a creased brown suit. In fact, everything about him looked creased. His lapels curled, the collar of his shirt appeared in need of starching. A tracery of lines surrounded his tired blue eyes. More lines corrugated his high forehead, from which a head of thick, curly brown hair swept back in an untidy spill. His mustache was an untrimmed soup-strainer, his jaw ill-defined. He was probably in his early forties, Will thought, but he looked much older.

'Help you?' he asked.

'I do believe you can, Mr. Cody. Ned Buntline's my handle. Here.' He passed Will a card. It identified Buntline as a correspondent for the *New York Weekly*. 'Magazine sent me out here to write an article on General Sheridan . . . and *you*, Mr. Cody.'

'Me?'

'Your exploits have carried even to the East, sir.'

'My reputation as a killer, you mean?'

Buntline raised his eyebrows. 'As a *plainsman*, sir. And our readers would like to know more about you.' He hesitated a moment, then said, his voice thick with the nasal twang of New York: 'Perhaps we could repair to one of this town's many drinking parlors and I could ask you a few questions?'

'What kind of questions?'

'You're a famous man, Mr. Cody. Why, the whole country wants to hear all about Buffalo Bill.'

Will began to shake his head. He really wasn't interested, not then and likely not ever. All he wanted to do was swap the ridiculous clothes he'd taken to wearing for the comfortable practicality of his old buckskins, then find a different line of work and reclaim some of the decency he felt he'd lost.

Then the germ of an idea came to him and he gave Buntline a closer appraisal.

'Seems to me I've heard of you,' he

said. 'You've written other stuff, too. Stories, I mean.'

'I have indeed, Mr. Cody. *The Mysteries and Miseries of New York, The Night of the Black Flag, The Maid of Monterrey, The Beautiful Nun, Navigator Ned, The Black Avenger* . . . all are mine, sir, and have elevated me to a position of great wealth and no small influence. Why, I daresay I could do the same for you — novelize your heroic exploits, I mean, and — '

'They haven't been very heroic just lately,' interrupted Will. 'But . . . '

'Yes, sir?'

'If I tell you somethin', Mr. Buntline . . . will your magazine print it?'

'They might.'

'All right,' said Will. 'You tell your readers this. The white man's got to stop killin' off the buffalo.'

Buntline forehead corrugated still more. 'Excuse me?'

'If we don't, they'll be wiped out. Gone forever . . . an' the Indian with 'em.'

286

Buntline shook his head. 'I don't follow, Mr. Cody. Why would that necessarily be a bad thing?'

'Did you love your mother, Mr. Buntline?'

'Well . . . I ran away from home when I was but a boy.'

'All right, I'll put it another way. Did you . . . appreciate . . . all the little things she did for you before you ran away?'

'I . . . yes sir, I suppose I did.'

'And after you ran away, did you miss her? The way she looked after you, I mean?'

Buntline hesitated, then nodded.

'Well, that's how it'll be with the buffalo, Mr. Buntline. Time was, we could number them in the millions. Tens of millions. Now I understand that you'll be countin' them in their thousands before much longer. Then it'll be a few hundred, a hundred, an' then maybe finally ten or fifteen. An' when they're gone, that's it. There's no way back.'

'But General Sherman says that one dead buffalo equals one dead Indian. Isn't that a *good* thing?'

The remark hit Will like an open hand. 'Forget it,' he said, losing patience. 'I got nothin' more to say to you, Mr. Buntline.'

He turned away, but Buntline caught him by the arm. 'Not so hasty, Mr. Cody! You must understand. This . . . well, it isn't what I was expecting — especially from a man whose own total number of kills is — '

'Four thousand, two hundred and eighty,' Will said tightly. 'And trust me, I regret every one. And you know *why*, Mr. Buntline? Because I knew better. I *knew* it was wrong. I knew that when I was ten or twelve years of age.' And all at once he was back around that camp fire with Hickok, and Bridger, and Carson. 'The Indian, he lives *with* life, Mr. Buntline. He don't try to scalp it flat, like us whites. If we took to the natural way of things, like the Indian, we might still save a little somethin' for

288

the generations that ain't been born yet.'

'But it's made you famous.'

'And it's made the Indian hungry.' He studied the smaller man. 'You're not writin' any of this down, mister.'

'Whether what you say is true or not, I'm not sure it's what our readers want to hear.'

'I'm not interested in what they want to hear. I'm only interested in making them understand the way it *is*. Then maybe we can stop it before it's too late.' He drew a breath, realizing the hopelessness of his cause. 'Jim Bridger put it best. He said that findin' an' seein' was the important thing . . . then leavin' everything just like it was . . . untouched.'

Then his voice and manner sharpened noticeably.

'You *still* ain't writin', Buntline.'

Buntline squared his heavy shoulders. 'No . . . And I'll tell you why, Mr. Cody. Because it sounds to me like you're on the red man's side.'

'Is that a bad thing?'

'If you're standing up for the red man, you're setting yourself against your own kind, surely?'

'Why can't I do what's right for both?'

'Well . . . ' Buntline began uncertainly.

Will lost patience again. 'Hobble your lip, Buntline. I don't want to hear anymore out of you. But it seems to me you could've had yourself a hell of a story.' He swung around and left the lobby.

Buntline hurried out onto the street after him. Paying him no mind, Will stepped astride his horse and turned it away from the hitch rail.

'Mr. Cody, wait up a moment! There're still some questions I want to — '

But Will just walked his horse away, suddenly knowing what he had to do to spread the word, and sitting all the straighter because of it.

Watching him go, Buntline shook his

head. A great opportunity — the chance to interview Buffalo Bill Cody himself — had just slipped through his fingers. But his disappointment lasted only seconds. It was as his editor always said: invention was the surest form of history.

Part Seven — Hero

25

Will rode directly to the telegraph office, which was enclosed in a large canvas wall tent. The telegrapher, an emaciated man in his forties with a green eyeshade and sleeve garters, looked up from a paper-cluttered desk and nodded howdy.

'Want you to send a telegram to the U.P. for me,' Will told him.

'Ten words will cost you twenty cents,' said the telegrapher.

'I'll take sixty cents' worth.'

The telegrapher took out a yellow form and a stub of pencil, licked the tip of the pencil and said: 'What's your message?'

'Just this,' Will said. 'Stop all advertising of buffalo shooting from trains. Supply no more weapons or ammunition to anyone. If not, Buffalo Bill promises to shoot the next passenger he sees killing buffalo.'

Startled by the message, the operator looked up at him. 'W-What the heck . . . ?'

'Send it, mister.'

'I can't send *that* — '

Will drew his Colt — the same Dragoon Wild Bill had given him the day they buried Lyle Reese. 'You'd better.'

The operator examined him more closely. 'Are *you* Buffalo Bill? Like it says in the message?'

'Yep.'

'All right,' said the telegrapher. 'I'm sendin'.'

And he began to tap the key with a hand that shook.

★　★　★

Will took his ease from a slope overlooking the U.P. rails that sliced through the prairie like a silver scar. Beside him sat a canteen of water and a hunk of cheese. He badly wanted whiskey but was trying to quit drinking. The day was fine and bright, with a stiff wind rippling the tall prairie grass, making it ebb and flow like waves on an ocean.

For the first time in a long while, he felt halfway at peace. The plains, this was home to him. Life was nowhere near as complicated out here. A man could breathe, and stretch, and grow. Most of all, he could still enjoy the wonder of the great open spaces while they were still there.

His mother had said he would be famous one day. He wondered now if she'd meant famous or infamous? But she'd said something else: that everyone would praise him.

He hoped that folks would praise him for what he had planned for today.

Name'll be in the history books, she'd said. *Be remembered forever . . . just like kings 'n' queens 'n' presidents . . .*

Going to make me'n your pa so proud, Will.

He hoped so.

Many years before, Wild Bill Hickok had told him to take every opportunity that came along. He had done so. But not all opportunities were good ones, as he now knew. Still, if a man made a mistake, there was only one thing he could do about it, and that was set things back to rights again.

He chewed the cheese, swallowed and washed it down with another mouthful of water. In the distance, a train whistle wailed mournfully across the plains.

Knowing he must make a move at last, he climbed to his feet and brushed himself down.

And that was when a voice behind him said: 'Not so fast, Will.'

For a moment he froze. Then, recognizing the voice, he turned, cautiously, and stared twenty feet up the gentle incline at the man who had the drop on him, silhouetted now against the harsh blue sky.

'Hello, Bill,' he said softly.

Wild Bill came down the slope toward him, one of his twin Navy Colts out and aimed squarely at Will's belly.

Now that the sun was no longer behind him, Will could see how the years since that dawn in Lawrence had changed his friend. Wild Bill was still as tall and lean as ever — still handsome, too, if it came to that. But there was also a raddled, dissipated quality to him that hadn't been there before. Though still a force to be reckoned with Wild Bill was getting soft, and too damn' fond of whisky, women and cards.

In a sudden flash of insight, it came to Will that one or all three would eventually kill Hickok off if he didn't change his ways.

He realized also that the booze had taken its toll on *him*, as well.

'That's a hell of a way to greet a man,' he said, gesturing toward the Colt.

Hickok looked uncomfortable. 'Well, they tell me you've gone a mite crazy.'

'Who does?'

'Sheridan. He says you've become an Indian-lover.'

'An' we all know how Sheridan feels

about the Indians.'

'Lot of folks feel that way about the Indians,' said Wild Bill. 'One of them is a feller by the name of Buntline. Seems you and he had a conversation that he took to be 'un-American'. He reported it to the Department of the Missouri in general an' to Sheridan hisself in particular. Sheridan was of a mind to ignore it until you sent that message of yourn to the U.P. Then he put *me* on your trail.'

'To stop me?'

'That's the size of it.'

'Then you and me got a problem, Bill.'

'Not if you forget such nonsense.'

'It's not nonsense. You ought to know that better than anyone.'

Wild Bill looked off across the plains. 'You think I *don't* know?' he asked. 'Hell, we're lucky to've kept the country like it is for as long as we have. But what can you do? What can one man do?'

'That depends on the man.'

'Whatever you got planned, Will . . . I

can't let you do it.'

'So stop me.'

Something in Will's eyes seemed to flatten down. It was the look of a man who was ready to kill or be killed, and Wild Bill reflected it perfectly.

'Remember the day we buried Lyle Reese,' said Will. 'Remember what you said to me when you gave me Reese's gun? This gun, right here?'

Hickok thought a moment, then said: 'Remind me.'

'You said Reese didn't have any more use for it, but maybe I might, if I went on to live the kinda life you thought I would.'

'I said that, did I?'

'Sure did. But I bet you never thought it'd come to this.'

'It doesn't *have* to come to this.'

'Then let me ride on down an' meet that train,' said Will. 'Let me go down there an' do what I got to do, and that's it, I swear it. I'll go my way and you go yours, and no one has to get hurt.'

Wild Bill thought about that for a

moment. 'What is it you got to do?' he asked carefully.

'It's all very simple,' Will replied. 'The work of a few minutes, that's all. And when I'm done, and that train down there reaches the end of the line, the word will spread far and wide, and then everyone will know that we got to stop the slaughter.'

Wild Bill's expression gave no hint as to what he was thinking as he stared at Will. Then, with a flourish, he spun his Colt and tucked it under his crimson sash.

'Damn,' he said, and when he grinned he was the old Wild Bill again, the one Will had grown up admiring. 'You always was a showman at heart.'

'This ain't for show.'

'As you say. But what the hell? Whatever it is, let's do it together. Truth to tell, I'm curious to see exactly what you got in mind.'

Relaxing, Will scooped up his canteen and the hunk of cheese. He threw the cheese to Wild Bill. 'Come on, let's go meet the train.'

Hickok went back up and over the slope, returning a few moments later with his horse, a chestnut with a white blaze on his face. Will swung into leather and they walked their mounts down toward the distant tracks stirrup to stirrup.

Hickok chewed thoughtfully on the cheese for a while, then said: 'Good cheese. Knowed this widow woman once, had this farm outside a St. Joe . . . Homely as a bog, she was, but she made the damnedest cheese . . . 'til the cow died. Never went back after that . . . ' leastways, not sober.'

The train was on the horizon now, showing black against the sky behind it. The big Baldwin 4–4–0 was belching smoke and making the rails ahead of it sing. Reining in beside the track, Bill pulled his slicker from behind his cantle and shook it out. It stirred a memory in him; of turning the herd of stampeding buffalo the day Ira Thomas died.

Then he waved the bright yellow garment over his head to attract the attention of the train's driver.

'What're you gonna do if he don't stop?' asked Wild Bill.

'*He'll* stop.'

Wild Bill laughed. 'Still think you know it all, don't you?'

The train came closer, and now Will could make out the tender, two maroon-colored Pullmans, the caboose, all rattling and swaying behind it. Nearer at hand, the rails began to creak and grind. But if anything, the train seemed to be gathering pace.

'Five dollars says he rolls right on by,' said Hickok.

'*Ten* dollars says you can't keep your mouth shut for the next five minutes.'

'Might touchy, ain't you?'

'Must be somethin' to do with you, Wild Bill. I'm not like it around anyone else.'

Wild Bill started to laugh some more, then abruptly stopped. 'I'll be damned,' he breathed. 'Looks like I owe you five bucks. That damn' train *is* slowin' down!'

It was true. While it was still about five hundred yards out, the train hitched a little as the brakes were applied. Will waved his slicker harder. The brakes squealed and the line of carriages slowed still further, the engine itself appearing almost to float on a cushion of steam as the distance shrank to three hundred yards, then two hundred, then just fifty.

With a screeching of brakes, the train stopped, crouching on the rails like a panting beast.

Stuffing the slicker back behind his cantle, Will walked his horse alongside the track, Wild Bill right behind him. The engineer and fireman poked their heads out of the cab, faces heat-red and sweaty.

'What's wrong?' asked the engineer, a thin man in round, wire-framed spectacles. 'Why'd you flag us down?'

Will drew rein and looked up at him. 'This an excursion train?'

'It sure is.'

'Thought as much.' He dismounted and handed his reins up to Wild Bill. 'You set right where you are, driver. I got business with your passengers.'

The engineer frowned. 'Who the hell are you?'

'I'm Buffalo Bill Cody.'

The engineer's face went slack. 'Saints alive — it *is* you!'

Will walked past the tender and paused at the steps leading up to the platform of the first Pullman. Wild Bill felt a twinge of misgiving as Will drew his Colt and then vanished into the coach.

What the hell is that boy fixin' to do?

There was no immediate answer. For a minute or so, nothing happened. Then he heard some raised voices, but couldn't distinguish individual words.

Silence fell again, but for the shushing of the idling engine.

'Are we bein' robbed, mister?' asked the fireman.

Before Wild Bill could reply, the

coach windows began to open, one by one, and disgruntled passengers began to toss out the weapons and ammunition that had been supplied by the U.P. Long guns, handguns and bullets clattered and alongside the tracks.

It was the same story with the second coach.

Wild Bill, now grinning from ear to ear, shook his head. 'No,' he replied at last. 'You ain't bein' robbed, fireman. You're bein' taught a lesson.'

Down at the far end of the train, Will hopped down and slid his Colt away. The conductor jumped from the caboose with a rifle in his hands and the two exchanged words. Then, under Will's direction, the conductor tossed his rifle aside and they started to work their way back up to the engine, stopping every so often to gather up the discarded rifles and handguns and lay them slantwise across the tracks.

At last they reached the engine, where Will took his reins back from Wild Bill and indicated that the conductor join his companions in the cab.

Remounting, he told the engineer: 'Whenever you're ready, you can move out.'

The engineer's mouth opened and closed as he fought for the right words and came up empty.

'You can move *out*,' Will repeated firmly.

The engineer went back to his wheels and levers, and after a time steam spurted from the blast pipes and slowly, slowly the train began to move again, twisting and crushing the weapons out of shape beneath its massive iron wheels.

'Sheridan ain't gonna like this,' Hickok noted as the train went on its way, growing smaller with distance.

'As you say,' Bill allowed. 'But those to come *will*.'

'You got a point there, Will. Damned if you ain't.'

Side by side, they galloped off across the seemingly endless grassland, leaving only laughter in their wake.

Authors' Note

The foregoing novel recounts events in the life of Buffalo Bill Cody as they were, and as we, the authors, would have liked them to be. Where the truth didn't always make for the best story, we were liberal in our use of Artistic License.

However, that should not be taken as any criticism of our subject.

At the height of his fame, Buffalo Bill was the most recognizable celebrity in the world.

He married Louisa Frederici in 1866 and fathered four children, two of whom died in infancy.

After thirty-eight years, he filed for divorce, claiming that Louisa had tried to poison him.

Following a reconciliation of sorts, they remained married for fifty-one years.

Buffalo Bill was featured in more than five hundred dime novels, beginning in 1869 with *Buffalo Bill, The King of the Border Men*, written by Ned Buntline.

In 1872, he made his stage debut opposite Texas Jack Omohundro in *The Scouts of the Prairie*, produced by Ned Buntline.

The following year, he and Omohundro were joined by his old friend, Wild Bill Hickok.

Also in 1872, Bill received the Medal of Honor for gallantry in action during the Indian Wars. In 1917 — the year of his death — the guidelines were changed so that only military personnel were eligible for the award. Consequently, his medal, and those of many other civilian scouts, was revoked.

In his now-legendary *Buffalo Bill's Wild West* show that was formed in 1882, Will shared the bill at one time or another with Annie Oakley, Sitting Bull and Calamity Jane Canary.

Buffalo Bill's Wild West show was

part of the American exhibition at Queen Victoria's Golden Jubilee in London in 1887.

The show also opened the World's Columbian Exposition in Chicago in 1893.

It toured Europe until 1906.

In 1896, Buffalo Bill helped develop the town of Cody, Wyoming.

In 1914, he founded The Col. W.F. Cody Historical Pictures Company to make short films about the Indian Wars.

He even acted in movies himself — in *The Circus Girl's Romance*, in 1915.

Since 1922, he has been portrayed in more than seventy TV and movie productions.

At the time of this writing, a new movie about Buffalo Bill is planned for 2017 — the centenary of his death.

The *Buffalo Bills*, the NFL football team named after him, started playing in 1960.

In 1988, he was honored with the first of two U.S. postage stamps.

The following year, after twelve years of investigation, the Army Board for the Correction of Military Records decided that Buffalo Bill was entitled to the Medal of Honor after all. The award was reinstated.

IN THE NAME OF JUSTICE
SHOOTOUT IN CANYON DIABLO
LONELY RIDER
A BULLET FOR LAWLESS
DEATH RIDES A PINTO
QUICK ON THE DRAW

By Ben Bridges:
MARKED FOR DEATH
HELL FOR LEATHER
MEAN AS HELL
DRAW DOWN THE LIGHTNING
HIT 'EM HARD!
DAY OF THE GUN
FIVE SHOTS LEFT
THE SILVER TRAIL
RIDING FOR JUSTICE

We do hope that you have enjoyed reading this large print book.

Did you know that all of our titles are available for purchase?

We publish a wide range of high quality large print books including:
Romances, Mysteries, Classics
General Fiction
Non Fiction and Westerns

Special interest titles available in large print are:
The Little Oxford Dictionary
Music Book, Song Book
Hymn Book, Service Book

Also available from us courtesy of Oxford University Press:
Young Readers' Dictionary
(large print edition)
Young Readers' Thesaurus
(large print edition)

For further information or a free brochure, please contact us at:
Ulverscroft Large Print Books Ltd.,
The Green, Bradgate Road, Anstey,
Leicester, LE7 7FU, England.
Tel: (00 44) **0116 236 4325**
Fax: (00 44) **0116 234 0205**

The mining town of King Creek sits in the heart of the Nevada goldfields. It has no law to speak of but Stover's Law — ruthlessly enforced by one greedy woman, her three callous sons, and a dozen hired gunmen. The Stover family is systematically fleecing the townsfolk of everything they have, with anyone standing in their way either bought off — or killed off. In desperation, Pearl Denton turns to her old friend, legendary town-tamer Sam Judge, for help . . .

SAVAGE

Jake Henry

In 1864, Captain Jeff Savage is tasked with taking down Carver's Raiders, a ruthless bunch of killers who have blasted a bloody path through the Shenandoah Valley. The mission is a failure, and Carver escapes with a handful of men. Two years later, he and his gang rob a bank in Summerton, murdering Savage's wife Amy. Several outlaws escape in the aftermath: armed with their names, Savage sets out to track each one down and exact his revenge . . .

THE SHOESTRINGERS

C. J. Sommers

Benjamin Trout, foreman of the K/K Ranch, has been cut loose for being too old — while Eddie 'Dink' Guest, a new hire, has been fired for being too young. With nowhere to go, both ride out together to seek work elsewhere. When they encounter widowed Beth Robinson and her daughter Minna in the wilderness, they are invited back to the women's ranch — and become the Robinsons' allies in the struggle to save their land from the predatory Cyrus Sullivan.